CW01627251

THE RETURN TO REASON SERIES
BOOK THREE

THE STORY SOWN FAR
Short Stories for Towering Times

THE RETURN TO REASON SERIES

THE STORY SOWN FAR
Short Stories for Towering Times
BOOK 3

THE RETURN TO REASON SERIES

Published by Bite Size Books 2023
Bite-Sized Books Ltd 16 High Holborn, London, WC1V 6BX, England
Registered in the UK. Company Registration No: 9395379

ISBN: 978-1-7393107-8-3

Cover Designs by Amelia Costley
Cover Photographs by Max Reeve

THE STORY SOWN FAR
Short Stories for Towering Times

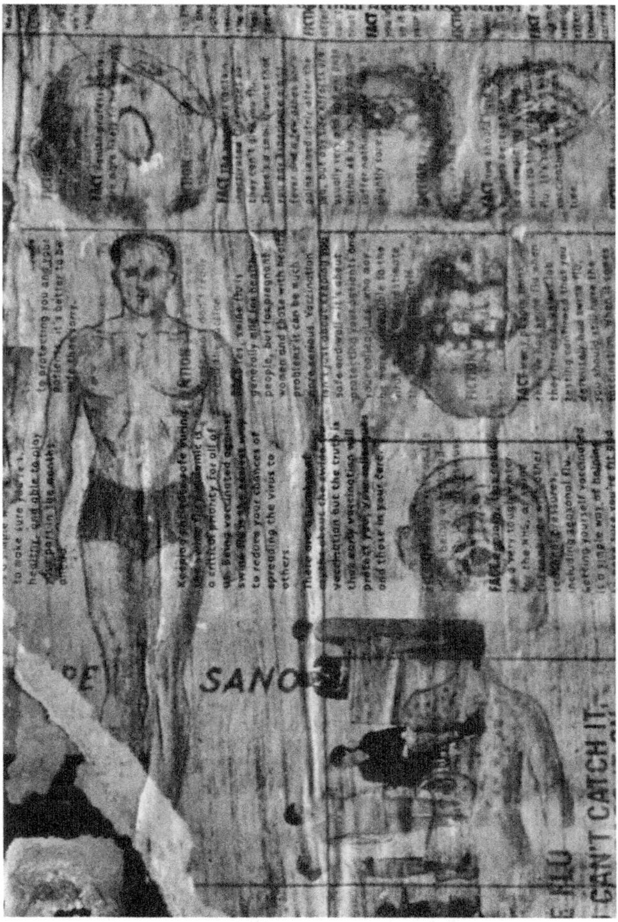

© Max Reeves

The six books in this series are each dedicated and in debt to the generosity of Bite Sized Books Publisher Julian Costley and to that of the artists featured within, whose work has allowed what you hold in your hand to come into being. The tried and tested phrase 'Without Whom,' has never been more pertinent. All writers are listed here alongside the number of the book which contains their work. I therefore wish to both thank and commend:

LISA AZARMI – Book 1
NICK BARTH – Book 1
CHRIS BOWSHER – Book 1
PETE BROWN – Book 1
RICHARD CABUT – Book 1, 2, 3, 5
CAT CATALYST – Book 1
AMELIA COSTLEY – Cover Design Books 1, 2, 3, 4, 5, 6
JULIAN COSTLEY – Book 1
LAYLA CURR – Book 3
GIL DE RAY – Book 3
UNICA FALLABLE – Book 2
GEOFF FRANCIS – Book 1
BENJIE FRASER – Book 1
SARABJEET GARCHA – Book 1
JULIE GOLDSMITH – Book 1
YALE GOULD – Book 3
JOHN HANEY – Book 1
LAUREN HARPER – Book 1, 5
JAN HERMAN – Book 1
JOHN HIGGS – Book 2
NICK HORGAN – Book 1
MICHAEL HOROVITZ – Book 1, 3
JAY JEFF JONES – Book 1
SHELLIE KELLY – Book 1
ANDREW KÖTTING – Book 6

EDEN KÖTTING – Book 6
ROSE LEVINSON – Book 2
LARS LINEFLIGHT – Book 6
TOMMY MARKS – Book 3, 5
NIALL McDEVITT – Book 1, 2, 5
GAVIN McGARVEY – Book 3
STEPHEN MICALEF – Book 1
ROBERT MONTGOMERY – Book 1
SAVITRI PEMA – Book 1, 3
CHRIS PETIT – Book 6
MANUELA RAYBAN – Book 4
CARLYLE REEDY – Book 3
MAX REEVES – Book 5, Cover photos Book 1, 2, 3, 4, 5, 6
MALCOLM RITCHIE – Books 1, 2, 3
JO ROACH – Book 1
DAVID RUSSELL – Book 1, 3, 5
GEOFF SAUNDERS – Book 3
AMELIA SCIANDRA – Book 5
IAIN SINCLAIR – Book 2, 6
HILARY SPIERS – Book 1, 3, 5
MARGARET D. STETZ – Book 1
VANESSA VIE – Book 1
SAIRA VIOLA – Book 1, 3
JAN WOOLF – Book 3, 5
JEFF YOUNG – Book 3, 5, 6

CONTENTS

THE RETURN TO REASON SERIES

THE RETURN TO REASON SERIES FOREWORD:

FORWARDS

The Return to Reason project comprises six books intended as a continuing series of selections, anthologies and single authored works aimed at defining what alternatives for a changing culture and society could be. These first six titles include contributions from a range of established writers and artists, alongside a handful of emergent practitioners, across each of the creative forms. They are an attempt to redefine what we want from art in general and reading in particular. At a time when it is impossible to sit on a bus or train – or in some cases, even a car – without seeing everyone immersed or captivated by a phone, our intention is to re-introduce the kind of exploration that only a special book can provide.

From poetry to short plays, stories, essays, freer forms and photography as narrative, these titles make a unique contribution. They are intended to work aesthetically, practically and in terms of content, and to enliven the time spent reading and engaging with them. As you move from the demanding to the accessible, it is hoped that you will become aware of what even the most limited of forms can accomplish, and of how truthfully a range of voices you may not be familiar with can speak to and communicate with you.

The last few years has seen mainstream society move away from the creative impulse in favour of the commercial. We therefore ask you to dip your toe into deeper waters that have been flowing around that shallow river as forcefully as ever. You will feel energised and refreshed if you do so, and it is hoped that this will then whet your appetite for the range of artistic delicacies Bitesize books has prepared for you.

Each contributor has gifted me with their work and for that I am eternally grateful. Where I have balanced with my own contributions, I can only state that I am both rolling the ball, while also laying the foundation for other fresh towers to rise. I hope that the view from the construction site is appealing and that as you examine the brickwork you find your own stairs to climb.

Here is why.

David Erdos
Series Editor London, June 2023

THE STORY SOWN FAR: An Introduction:

I'll keep this short, and perversely, in the form of a poem,
As to capture the intent of short stories is as elusive,
Perhaps as good verse. For a good short story should shine
And validate its small format. It should, in vignette
Vouchsafe and value the currency contained in the purse

That the writer expends in order to capture in passing
The scene, situation, or summoned world, fast as dreams.
Each story here achieves this and each extends
The known limit. Tommy Marks' tiny tales prise death
Open, while Jeff Young's performance text is all story

As each paragraph parades life's lost schemes.
Saira Viola's Punk Noir is a neon street streaked by murder,
Richard Cabut's Dark entries and search for a kiss
Glistens grime. While the great Michael Horovitz
Bequeathes his last breath across fragments from the kiss

Of life that restores him, as Jan Woolf, Hilary Spiers,
David Russell, Val Vassay, Carlyle Reedy, David Bramwell,
Geoff Saunders, Yale Gould and Savitri Pema paint icons
Of a more personal type for harsh times. All this, and parts

1-3 of Gil De Ray's Voodootron, with its dystopian dream
Dipped in mushrooms. Meanwhile, real scenes and Heathcote's
Heists from Malcolm Ritchie's life story conjure the mind's
Rueful magic, while Gavin McGarvey's micro-tales
Trap behaviour, and Layla Curr re-examines the spectacular

Fall of a King, who has been condemned by his cock,
Making a pen from his penis, As well as the instrument
For all organs and a vast range of voices to empower
These tales and so, sing. Indeed. the short story as song
Is an interesting notion. It is not about yarns, or, twists,

But new reasons to re-engage and to read,
And thereby construct a new tower for words,
Better for us than the Babel that allegedly informed
Language and the rooms where its practised.
Here, then, are stories which are teaching us all

What we need.

David Erdos
June 2023

TOMMY MARKS:

TWO GHOST STORIES:

Ch-ch-Changes

David Bowie just called. Apparently, the new album is finished. After sixty-nine years rehearsal, he has been overjoyed to discover an entirely new frequency.

Little Chef

Close to Birmingham, the ghost of Peter Cook has been seen at a Motorway Service Station. It was heard to cry, ''Where is Dudley?' again and again, through the rain.

JEFF YOUNG:

A552 HEX: TRANSLATING THE STREETS FRANK CAVANAGH'S SHOE REPAIRS

(Originally, a sound installation by Jeff Young and Martin Heslop as part of 'Translating the Street', Saturday 5th March 2016, 10.30am- 5.00pm, Frank Cavanagh's Shoe Repairs, 369 Borough Road, Birkenhead.)

A spell against the dual carriageway.

Behind every rusted shutter on Borough Road there are ghosts…the ghosts of shopkeepers, of bakers and men selling sweets. Behind every boarded up window there are dead people laughing lightly, they are there like a memory we cannot quite retrieve…but if you listen closely, listen through the sound of passing traffic, perhaps you can hear them whisper that they lived here, they worked here, they passed the time of day with old widows and young lovers and they had a story…if we listen, maybe we can hear their stories, above the roar of engine noise and maybe we can silence the dual carriageway with a magic spell…

Bring
your
shoes to
Frank's!'

A552 Hex

1)

This is a Hex against a wound, pulling the power up from cables beneath the street and stealing the air from speeding cars, words caught up in the slipstream of haulage trucks, a spell cast against the A552, cursed dual carriageway, a shout against traffic-roar, a howl against abandonment and managed decline…

2)

It begins with a pair of boots, soles broken, leather cracked. I take them to Frank Cavanagh's Shoe Repairs at 369 Borough Road, Birkenhead. The cobbler doesn't think much of the boots or the man who last repaired them. He charges me nine quid and at first he doesn't want to tell his stories. Who can blame him? Who am I to come walking into his shop with mad ideas of magic?

3)

As I walk down Oxton Road, I stop at the site of Karl Deuschle's pork butchers shop, where in May 1915 people rioted, ransacked the shop and incinerated the contents in revenge for the sinking of the Lusitania. On one street corner there is a gutted pub in ruins and nearby there is the smell of roasted chestnuts coming from a fruit and veg shop. I nearly go inside a 'Free Wi Fi Available' pub with no name but instead I walk on, looking for Malcolm Lowry books in junk shops and wondering where Charlie Chaplin drank when he walked these streets a hundred years ago…

4)

Science fiction flyover curving over the chimney pots of abandoned boozers and nite-spots…a man up there in an overcoat like a fallen angel in 'Wings of Desire'…I walk through the shopping centre, looking for the Hippodrome Music Hall and find it in T.K Maxx, where the ghost of Vesta Tilley singing 'Burlington Bertie' can be heard above the sound of a 70's pop star wishing it could be Christmas every day…

5)

Look at that Pathe News footage of searchlights arcing across the night. It's 1949 and Gregory Peck's dazzling, Hollywood smile is lighting up the Ritz cinema at the world premier of Forsyte Saga. When Peck sings 'Auld Lang Syne' everything seems possible. But the luminous night twinkles in Margaret Lockwood's eyes, where we glimpse her premonition of dead cinemas, Birkenhead's palaces of dreams reduced to rubble and car parks, rotting bingo parlours, dodgy pool halls, gutted hulks…

6)

Behind every rusted shutter on Borough Road there are ghosts…the ghosts of shopkeepers, of bakers and men selling sweets. Behind every boarded up window there are dead people laughing lightly, they are there like a memory we cannot quite retrieve…but if you listen closely, listen through the sound of passing traffic, perhaps you can hear them whisper that they lived here, they worked here, they passed the time of day with old widows and young lovers and they had a story…if we listen, maybe we can hear their stories, above the roar of engine noise and maybe we can silence the dual carriageway with a magic spell…

7)

Walking is political. The dual carriageway doesn't want us to walk so our footsteps are subversive. What if we stopped the traffic? What if we walked into the six lanes of cars and just said let's call it a day, and declared an imaginary Borough Road where the Rubicon stream flows...

8)

Walking is literature. Every pair of shoes has a story to tell. Every pair of trainers hanging off the phone wires; every pair of walking boots; every pair of blue suede shoes; every pair of dancing shoes; every pair of football boots; every pair of work shoes; every pair of high heel shoes that ever clattered into night clubs. Every crack in the leather, every worn down heel, every sweat stain and every split in the sole...every pair of shoes is a chapter in its owner's autobiography.

9)

'The shape of a city, as we all know, changes more rapidly than the shape of the human heart.'

C
h
a
rl
e
s
B
a
u
d
el
ai
r
e

The road is losing its memory…

10)

Malcolm Lowry swaggers down Grange Road, looking for a glimpse of the Mersey. I can see a jitter of panic in his eyes as he struggles to comprehend the labyrinth of the Pyramids Shopping Centre. He doesn't know he's a ghost and that the charity shops and chain stores were built on purpose. He drifts past Cash Converters, greetings card shops, pay day loan sharks and fly-by-night traders selling cack-handed tracksuits, down onto the A552 asphalt where he walks headlong into the glut of Transit vans puking out of the Mersey Tunnel's gob. He sings a fucked up shanty, sings a mad, shamanic curse against the violence inflicted on dirty old Birkenhead. Look at him, look at the ghost of Malcolm Lowry in the middle of Borough Road, singing a curse against our sins…

11)

The road is losing its memory, a kind of dementia. Drift-scattered, dragged along the wind corridors of Borough Road, away blow the memories, away blow the meaning and matter, away blow the fragments of romantic outings, of spring flowers dancing in Happy Valley.

12)

Forgetting is political. When a building grows old we witness it dying. We want it to survive but we feel powerless to save it. And when the time comes and it dies adorned in buddleia and fly posters we are stricken with nostalgia for the cinema we hardly ever visited, or for the old tiled butchers shop where we never bought meat. And then, when its gone we begin to forget what it even looked like. The building is erased from the street and from our imaginations, and that erasure of place and loss of memory is the plan. We are expected to forget and that is how they change the world without asking for permission.

13)

Memories of the people you love are supposed to last forever, but often they're the first to go.

J.G. Ballard,
The Kindness of Women

14)

This road is a cancellation of the very idea of place.

15)

Have you seen those old men who watch demolitions, heads shaking in sorrow as wrecking balls ruin? But soon we've forgotten the building that stood here: the market, the cinema and the pub on the corner. Then here comes the Retail Park and the by-pass and the death of the old men who used to be children.

16)

When we drive along the dual carriageway we are passing a film of abandoned souls, a dementia narrative, unspooling on a cinema screen stretching into infinity. We are watching the decay of memory, as if history was stored on unstable, nitrate based film stock and is slowly disappearing into mortar and brick. This is the only way to explain the madness of this vision of ruins.

17)

The broken Barbie Doll, wired to the railings, the petrol station bouquet dessicating in its cellophane wrapper, rain-blurred ink 'In Memoriam' card bubble gummed to a rose.

18)

'His whole being was drowning in memories, the smells of Birkenhead and of Liverpool were again heavily about him, there was a coarse glitter in the cinema fronts, children staring at him strangely from the porches of public-houses. Janet would be waiting for him at the Crosville bus stop, with her red mackintosh and her umbrella, while silver straws of rain gently pattered on the green roof…'Where shall we go? The hippodrome or the Argyle? … I've heard there's a good show on the Scala –'

Malcolm
Lowry
'Ultramar
ine'

19)

Caught up in the tail-winds
of passing delivery vans
and Ford Mondeos

Last utterances lost

Gutter-throats swallowing murmurs,
the gurgle and stutter of memory loss

20)

The act of walking this road is a magic spell. Slowly with never a pause plod on and never recede. Backs turned. Both bowed. Joined by holding hands. Plod on as one. One shade. Another shade. Samuel Beckett.

Walking suspends death

21)

Who sits on the Borough Road benches, looking beyond the passing cars to the town they cannot reach? A small heap of cigarette butts and scattered dust is carefully placed on the pavement like the cremation ashes of dreamers, laced with trace elements of petrol lead and sulphur. I sit here for five minutes, a memorial ritual for Catherine Glegg, who 180 years ago owned the meadow beneath the Borough Road tarmac. I breathe in the nitrogen dioxide and scratch a hex into the metal bench as the traffic thunders on through the Birkenhead murk…

22)

gutters run with rain-dirt   lost
memories washed away

the last remaining   fragments
of what used to be

of what used to have   meaning
of what will soon
no longer be here

all this will need
          rememberers
to keep the past alive through   ritual

by repeating certain   words
and naming certain   things

and naming certain   places
and celebrating certain   people
and mourning those who   died
and those that used to be   here

23)

To this day, every evening at dusk, Charlie Chaplin is walking down Argyle Street, on his way to the Theatre of Varieties, two shows nightly. To this day, W.C Fields is strolling down Grange Road in his 75-dollar suit, dusting cigar ash from his sable fur. To this day, Marie Lloyd is packing them in to Birkenhead's music halls and wooing the crowd with 'The Boy I Love Is Up In The Gallery'. To this day Dan Leno is drunk on the Seacombe landing stage and Malcolm Lowry is spitting in the Mersey and longing for deep water…

24)

Beneath six lanes of traffic there used to be spring flowers, on the banks of Happy Valley. The lost Rubicon stream is buried beneath the tarmac and a woman I speak to believes that when the storm drains overflow it's the Rubicon escaping from its earth-tomb. Heavy rain brings secret history to the surface in the form of ghost-water.

25)

I think the key image of the 20th century is the man in the motor car. It sums up everything: the elements of speed, drama, aggression, the junction of advertising and consumer goods with the technological landscape. The sense of violence and desire, power and energy; the shared experience of moving together through an elaborately signalled landscape. We spend a substantial part of our lives in the motor car, and the experience of driving condenses many of the experiences of being a human being…the marriage of the physical aspects of ourselves with the imaginative and technological aspects of our lives. I think the 20th century reaches its highest expression on the highway. Everything is there: the speed and violence of our age; the strange love affair with the machine, with its own death.

26)

Seventy years of working with his hands. Mending the shoes of how many hundreds of people? Frank Cavanagh in Birkenhead, working patiently surrounded by his tools, strips of leather, glue, nails. Telling stories, watching the road, having a pint and a gas in the Happy Valley pub. Watching the road...

27)

Graffitied Hex on steel shutters of Borough Road's derelict buildings, carved with old cobblers tools, scrawled with betting shop biros...just as a yellow blossom is a cure for jaundice or a root shaped like a foot is a remedy for gout, these words are folk medicine. I am walking against the traffic and these footsteps are a ritual curse...

28)

A poster for a show at the Argyle a hundred years ago, starring Fred Hastings, the Cowboy Ventriloquist and his Loquacious Friend Freddy.

A mangled wind up gramophone player in a junkshop summons up the ghost of George Formby, an apparition of him singing in 1921. And then he's gone…

Gone the way of gutted music halls and dead cinemas, the Ritz, the Gaumont, the Scala, The Empire, Astor, Coliseum, Palace, Plaza, Regal, Rialto, the Roxy and the Ritz. A scratched 78, a portal into a world of broken dreams.

29)

On the shutters of defeated shops I watch Super 8 home movies of children who are now old or dead, skipping ropes and spinning hula-hoops. Flickering visions of windows full of gramophone players, talking books, top hats in the gents outfitters and a dapper chap in a boater outside H.P Mann's Grocery and Provision Merchant. A boy is staring right into my eyes, reaching out to me from a hundred years ago and I almost feel I know him. This is a haunted memory cinema, a magic lantern show of disintegrating dreams…

30)

I am wearing a pair of brown brogue boots repaired by Frank Cavanagh. I walk along the eastern side of Borough Road. The road imposes limits on where we can walk but the walker breaks the limitation. Hobo alphabet stickers on lampposts and railings, mad scratchings, an outlaw highway code. Traffic on the A552 is at a standstill and I am the only thing moving. The hex is working.

31)

A deflating silver party balloon is anchored at the pelican crossing, dancing like the last hurrah of an abandoned hen night conga line.

32)

Birdsong. Children singing skipping songs. Marie Lloyd singing 'The Boy I Love Is Up In The Gallery. Gone. Forever, gone…

33)

I read somewhere that motorways are literally ballasted with stories. In every mile of motorway there are 45,000 buried books, holding the Tarmac and asphalt in place absorbing the roar of traffic. So the magic spell against a motorway is embodied within its own dark materials of bitumen and tar. What is the ballast of the A552? Is it remembering? Is it the voices of children? Is it the fragments of lives once lived here?

Illuminating the bitumen.

34)

This is a Hex against a wound, pulling the power up from cables beneath the street and stealing the air from speeding cars, words caught up in the slipstream of haulage trucks, a spell cast against the A552, cursed dual carriageway, a shout against traffic-roar, a howl against abandonment and managed decline...

This is a hex made by walking and trying to remember who was here.

MICHAEL HOROVITZ

UNSETTLED ACCOUNTS

UNSETTLED ACCOUNTS is a working title for many files of drafts from which I've excerpted non-sequentially, but sort-of chronologically, herewith. These drafts and other sources are functioning a bit like a painter's sketchbook, towards the completion of pictures in a personal retrospective; or, to skip the metaphor, towards a discursive autobiography, on the principle that an unexplained life has hardly been worth living.

DH Lawrence called the novel "the one bright book of life", but much as I love nearly all Lawrence's writing, I incline more to the view of Kenneth Patchen, that sometimes "Novelists talk about their characters because they've (so) little to say about themselves", although I don't find boundless narcissism appealing either. But I do like Patchen's notion that 'literature of the future should lay truth open on a higher level — one person telling another of the events in their own hearts".

My hope is that without contrived plots or theories I'll account for such personal experiences, inner and outer, as feel worth articulating.

The drafts (will) move from prose to poetry and back like the mind (as mine does, at least). The books I know which are close-ish to what I can envisage it might end up as, include Keats's Letters, Joyce's and Dylan Thomas's (self-)portraits, Patchen's Journal of Albion Moonlight, Allen Ginsberg's Journals, and the autobiographical volumes of Delacroix, Kathleen Raine, and Alan Ross. Though of course the adventure of writing and reading may largely consist of finding out (I hope) that mine may prove quite different from these —

January 1946

The evening sun came down much earlier o those post-war Fridays — not to sink the heart, then, as in St Louis Blues, nor as menacingly symbolic as Eliot's "patient etherised upon a table"— those moods were to come in my late teens. But the Friday dusk always fell with a heavy agenda — a safety curtain dropped against secular life, as if to shelter the private theatre-piece of our Jewish Sabbath from the unholy infectious atmosphere of the Gentiles around.

It went down extra early in midwinter, of course, when I was licensed to skip the entire afternoon of school. I wallowed in the privilege, felt to dreaming in the deserted lunchtime underground, dawdled in Hampstead's sleepier byways, and often got lost exploring various unguarded playgrounds and gardens. When I finally got home it was

— "Hurry up boy, 11 soon and still always last . . . Will you ever be a Man?

So, don't just stand there — tug off that weekday gear into Shabbos suit, Come On (stiff whiteness of shirt, tie chokingly braced to it, suit-of-armour jacket entered — nervous fingers splash hurry over face, slick down hair), we're going Now — don't try creeping in for last Kaddish pretending you've been there for the whole service . . . Nu, Goy — where is your Hat?"

Must wear a hat to synagogue . . . . At last, hanky pinned inside pocket, strenuously prepared for the Day of Rest . . . My white-bearded father and four older brothers truly sojourn this oasis of time, oasis from street-time and world value; but weird —thinking Good, here we are, the only smart people in the road of a Friday evening. The faithful few—fit to meet—hip to greet the radiant Bride of Sabbath.

What use our hymns and prayers? It's raining, all over North London I suppose. Lucky that about hats—not allowed to carry umbrellas; carrying anything taboo. But the reason I'm told isn't only that this would count as Work, but that you are always supposed to have something between you and God. — God?! Isn't he everywhere, not just an invisible power in heaven? And is heaven only in the sky? Will I dare ask the family such things? Some of them would say "Pisch, God is crying at your lack of faith". But isn't religion meant to get us closer to whoever, whatever God is, not more separate? Ah, but the God of the Jews is Jealous. Jealous of what, I wonder . . .

— Perhaps of how my hand likes it in father's greatcoat pocket . . . till, sigh, report on the week's work. Yes, yes, I got good marks. Don't tell about the panic or punishment in the showers. Not about my secret pre-dawn sledge rides down this same Oakhill Avenue, fresh snow glistening on squelchy leaves, ecstasy of sliding steady and smooth—then fetching up, a toy plane's happy landing, on the grass dip harbour at the bottom flanked by high hedges. I can see through them into the tennis court there — puddle-drenched tonight. Good to have a routine, walk the same way every week.

Tradition, consistency . . . but the people in most of these houses don't deliberately go out when it's pouring. . . What good is Good anyway? And his reasonable are the Reasons?

What I know is the dripping hat now weights a ton and is much harder Work than a brolly would be . . .

Darker. Rain, sleet and snow wildly swirling — but I don't want to bow to any of it — God or the elements — not with the Chosen Race, nor with the barren creaking council-trimmed trees. In defiance let me run the heath, flee the ritual — free with the others, not my grim brothers — Yes! Let me rather strike well away from this ghetto and run with dread heathens — like the scruffy Back Lane gang. Last week they let me tag along on one of their bombsite rampages. The ten of us scaled an impossibly high fence into forbidden grounds of the gaunt gothic Burgh Institute—to plunder it's air-raid-blitzed entrails.

Wind-shifting cubbyholes of tree and bush enclosed us, but we could see, in a clearing, the statues lined up in pairs as though for Oranges and Lemons — God knows why it's called that (the game's more like train carriages slowing down under the bridges).

. . . . Oh, maybe that's it, people like to think God knows when they do not, needing to feel Somebody knows? Well, I don't believe He can know so much if He's so busy being a Jealous God. Like those two bossy girls who broke up the most beautiful statue, a pierrot with sad face. On purpose —smashed him to bits. He'd stood for nobody knows how long undisputed — I had to jump out of the shadows then, make a garland of leaves and flowers to place on the split head — but it rolled away down a crater. The others shouted, "Hey — there was a Time Bomb down there", but I leapt down after it, had to make sure the head-piece of pierrot was safe. But where was it? So dark and gloomy there . . . My hands met shrapnel and crumbling wall-structures, but I couldn't see anything for ages. When my eyes got used to the dark I suddenly glimpsed a crouch shape in the far corner. "Statue, is it you?"— God, help, my god — a raincoated Man with his flies undone . . . wanking, till the spunk flew in an arc towards me — "It's alright sonny-jim, don't run away" . . . I clambered up terrified, leaving one shoe (pretended at home I'd left it for drowned in the Vale of Health pond)

. . . . "What is it?" the others yelled

— " I think there is a bomb down there"

1977 (In the Cotswolds)

No matter how late I've gone to sleep, I wake up I here at first light or earlier, instinctively aware that the cock will be crowing. So out I leap to raise the coop's portcullis, ark-angelic knight in shining armour — or more often, feeling more like the archetypal motherhen's mother — a bleary dressing- gown upon a stick . . .

I replenish their feed and wipe chickenshit off the drawbridge (chickenshit permeates every aspect of our lives), and watch the seven ladies troop out under the direction of his nibs, who pompously struts his stuff like some poultrified Toscanini or Mick Jagger astride the hopper. In the intervals of his by now utterly redundant alarums, I tune to stereo selections from the 'Today' programmes of other awakening creatures—and the farewell broadcasts of others again who're giving up the ghost to their exultant predators: worms turn over in voles, voles and field-mice in owls. The untameable aggro-cultural cycle.

The young bantams's eggs are the size of small testicles lately. Is it this thought which provokes heated runs to the bog so soon after eating two of them? Or can it be that the wild spinach and nettles I ate them with weren't properly cooked (. . .unlike the matzo balls in the Jewish joke about the traveller who steps off a plane in New York on Christmas Day: he's ravenous, but finds the only restaurant that's open near his hotel is a Kosher one. Never having tried Jewish food, he ask the waiter what's good, to be told that the Matzo Ball soup is perfection itself, for starters. When he's cleaned every drop from his plate with noisy relish, the waiter takes it and asks what he'd like next, to which the dinner replies: "What other parts of the Matzo do you cook?").

— Or maybe I accidentally garnished the dish with layers' mash, catfood — or bantams's droppings, even? Or perhaps I've got the runs because yesterday the bantams gobbled a huge fed of congealed Colonel Sanders's Kentucky Fried Chicken some visitors had brought much more of than any of us had appetite or room for; the bantams pounced and fought for every scrap of their own cooked kind as though it was the most delectable manna from chicken heaven . . .

'H'm" I muttered absently, "the bee is humming"—and my son, who's romped up to the pen, immediately ripostes: "The hum is being". It was mainly with him in mind that we moved out of London when he was still in nappies, hoping'll grow up unclouded by pollution, congestion, competition and the other jokes of Mammon. There have been many delights, including the dawning of his seventh birthday recently, at which we went down to the coop to find the seven hens had each laid one egg—happy egg-mass indeed.

But we were off-beams in hoping, in our thumbless ignorance, that we'd get virtually all our food for free.

One day 'You reap what you sow' may prove to be a reward and not a reproof. Thus far I'm still in debt for the coop, the run, the wire, the feed, the hopper, the transportation, the water bowl, gardening tools, manure, seedlings . . .

Mindful of last summer's potato blight, I planted twenty rows of spuds at enormous expense, leaving little room for anything else, back in March. Now they are avalanching faster that we can give them away. I'm told by the farmer to forget them as there's a national glut. Potatoes are ten a penny, where last year a bit un cost 10p. And last year we chucked several hundred apples, where now a small one costs more than a peach — and not a one's budding on our trees.

The crafty or constitutional slowness of Gloucestershire yokels used to irritate us before we lived here. Now we're locals we appreciate its necessity, if one is to breathe in time and harmony with the turning trees, still stones, and songs of the subtly shifting seasons. Nature's archaic logic — the poetry of the underground of the ultimate earth mother.

With birds in their heaven, all's well with the worms. The cut worm forgives the plough, as firewood the chain saw. And I know a bank where the wild thyme blows—on good days—thither we wend our toes, and the wild time there we have of it.

For where the bee sucks there suck I, warmed by the good earth breast's juices, high —

1980 (Oxford Revisited)

. . . . Ran into my old Moral Tutor from Oxford — in the College S. C. R. We drew our pens and crossed them, having fingered the thin silver arrows on the caps with nostalgic appreciation. 'Have a drink" he urged, solemnly decanting the contents of a full inkbottle into my glass. It beaded and bubbled at the brim. I must have eyed its Royal Blue hue somewhow nervously, for "— it's all right dear boy", he assured me, "it's guaranteed 99% Washable. Got it in '51 from Smiths' of the Corn. A very good year for Quink". He watched me quaff it (though God knows it tasted ughy as hell) till only the faintest stain of the dregs was left, with a Solv X-radiant inkling of sanctimonious satisfaction written all over his fat gleaming Permanent Red face.

—"Here's to Parker's"

I quipped, invoking not only the bookseller and of course the pen company, but also the pioneer bob saxophonist in order to feel one up—him being obviously too unhip to get this reference. But as if to prove me wrong, he then squirted two jets from his recharged pen down each of his nostrils, snorted down every drop, and emitted a high-pitched whinny—presumably to convey his sense of our complete mutual elevated and tasteful contentment. 'Well, must be going now. Going to Kansas City", he concluded: " So sorry that I can't take you" —and left, with thirty-four more bottles chunkily clinking in the depths of his grimy beige betoggled duffle-coat's humpy hood . . . .

April '95 (Mum's last Pesach)

Visited mum at Goldstar Old People's Home. Now that she's 100 and 7 months, she's decided to stay in there just for the Passover week. When I came in through the main entrance off Platts Lane, an old woman in a crumpled white muslin dressing gown seemed to be straining at the end of a string, like a dog tethered to its kennel.

The receptionist, Mrs Kaplan, said I'd find Mummy in the Sun Lounge. I was ushered through a long room whose walls were lined with chairs all around, oldies sat in most of them, several muttering to themselves, one wrestling with an invisible adversary. A giant TV set was the centrepiece of one wall. Most of the occupants were women ("Widows like me", Mum said later).

On passing the adjoining room, my heart leapt up to see her in the corner, almost the only person in the crowded sunlit glasshouse area involved in a dialogue with the others.

Through the tiniest if them, she was often standing up tremendously straight, with at least four of five others around her, reminding me of the most popular child in the school playground, in whose halo or aura others circled, keeping a reverent specs between them and her. It took her a minute to realise who I was, and then her first concern was to try to introduce me to her group — but though she knew their names, most of them seemed way beyond comprehending or carrying through such formality. Then Mum suggested we go to her room, found her stick and hobbled in front, guiding me to the lift. We went to her room on the top floor, which overlooks Finchley Road at its busiest intersection between Hampstead and Golders Green.

Shew asked me to close the window, and we sat and looked at one another. I was overwhelmed: it was the first time I'd seen her to sit down with a look at, alone, outside her house, for many years. I tried to stop myself from weeping, and she seemed not to notice.

She spoke, with her customary measured gentleness and precision, of the new routines in the home, and how everything was done for her, which made her "get lazy".

It was as though many years of our relationship (sixty this year) were peeled away. My eyes had difficulty in sustaining the meeting her upright steady gaze tacitly solicited — but just about managed, especially when she got talking again. Just one of the very few elderly men there apparently likes to sing, and speak of her beloved Jewish hymns and prayers before, during, and after meals.

We slowly went downstairs again, and passed through the main sitting room to go out for a brief but leisurely walk. The inmates were sat uneasily, looking sharply away from one another or at their feet, which were variously shod, slippered or bare. Most clutched into themselves like nervous, shy infants left to get on with it on their own at a party where they hardly knew any of the others, nor wanted to.

The man Mum sang with at meals waved to her amiably, reminding me of the story George Melly tells about a bloke at an Old Folks Home get-together who buttonholes the biddy he fancies with the gambit: "I bet you don't know my name, do you?" "Naw I dawn't" she replies (in a Northern accent), . . . "but if you ask Matron, I'm sure she'll be able to tell it you".

Mum looked at everything outside her wonted avid curiosity. Whenever she wanted to speak she halted, and fixed her bright sky-blue eyes on me. I tried to keep hold of her hand, but every moment she felt able to walk alone, she would grasp he stick fiercely, and do so.

It was a dazzling spring day; suddenly we found ourselves on Kidderpore Avenue suffused in white, pink, and gold light streaming down through the flocculent blossoms heaving and shimmering on a clump of high trees back from the road. Mum immediately stepped under them, inhaled deeply, and said the blessing for the first sight of blossoms this year. Then turned to go back to Goldstar.

She placed the warm cask of her tender hands round my bowed head, as she always did when we were about to part, and quietly blessed me. We kissed on each cheek at the Home's entrance, and I watched her go in to join the end of the long slowly lurching procession to lunch.

1: "Pesach"— Hebrew for 'Passover', annual eight-day feast [cf Easter] on which Jews commemorate the exodus of the Israelites from the captivity of Egypt, named after the destroying angel who passed over every dwelling occupied by Israelites whilst slaying the first-born of all Egyptians.

Orthodox Jews clear every crumb of leavened bread from their homes for the duration of this Festival, and install a complete array of alternative bread-free Kosher-for-Pesach diets and kitchenware—as my mother did until the spring following her hundredth birthday.

1997 (On the bus)

. . . . This dank hungover mid-December jingle-jungle morning I'm late for work, choked on indigestible government policies, clutching with at least 50 other filthy-tempered time-pawns to the cage-bar hand-rails of a so-called 'Golden Arrow' single-decker cattle-truck-type 31 bus that lurches sickening through convoluted crater-scarred roadwork-blockaded streets . . .

There's a long wait somewhere between Harrow Road and Kilburn.
— I need to get to Camden Town, but we're stuck for no apparent reason in the shadow of a looming derelict tower block. The cadaverous young female driver's just sitting in the cab varnishing her nails.

Britpop sizzles at irregular intervals from her leaky headphones.

When I chime in with a horde of other passengers who start moaning at her puh-leeze to get going, she shouts "That's it" and leaves the bus. I worm to the rear in low dungeon and sprawl a clumsy entree amidst the stinky gaggle of bums who've taken over the back seats alcove. Despite their shrill pissed hostility and retchings, my exasperation subsides into a cosy doze.

. . . but the very moment I'm about to ease into inner sanctum of my dream (continuous orgasm, gushingly reciprocated by the ultimate Immortal Beloved sex-bomb on mossy riverbank of a tropical paradise garden where all creatures lie down at ease with one another and get up to no bad) — I'm awoken by a hectic grinding of gears in a blizzard of fuuums-bo-wo-ro-the-tZeh—— ooorrgh . . . . It is the bus jerking into motion at last. Off we speed, with a surly middle-aged burly male at the wheel — but he's done a U-turn, I slowly apprehend, for the bus is racketing back in the wrong direction: in another 7 minutes or so we'll be at the World's End in King's Road, Chelsea. I also find I can't get up — the ceiling keeps getting lower and lower and I am forced, like Alice in the White Rabbit's bedroom, to lie flatter and flatter on the floor —

gradually realising there are no other passengers and this is in fact my coffin.

Everything starts blacking out, except one question faintly flickering . . . . Is the world to come any better?

A NOTE FROM THE EDITOR:

In the days following Michael Horovitz's sad passing in July 2021, his partner Vanessa Vie lovingly typed up these selections from an ongoing legacy of a life pressed into print. Combining typescripts and handwritten entries, these few pages form part of a grander and more romantic gesture, intended to kiss Michael back into life through the hand and the heart and the eye. It is an honour to be able to reproduce them here. (DE)

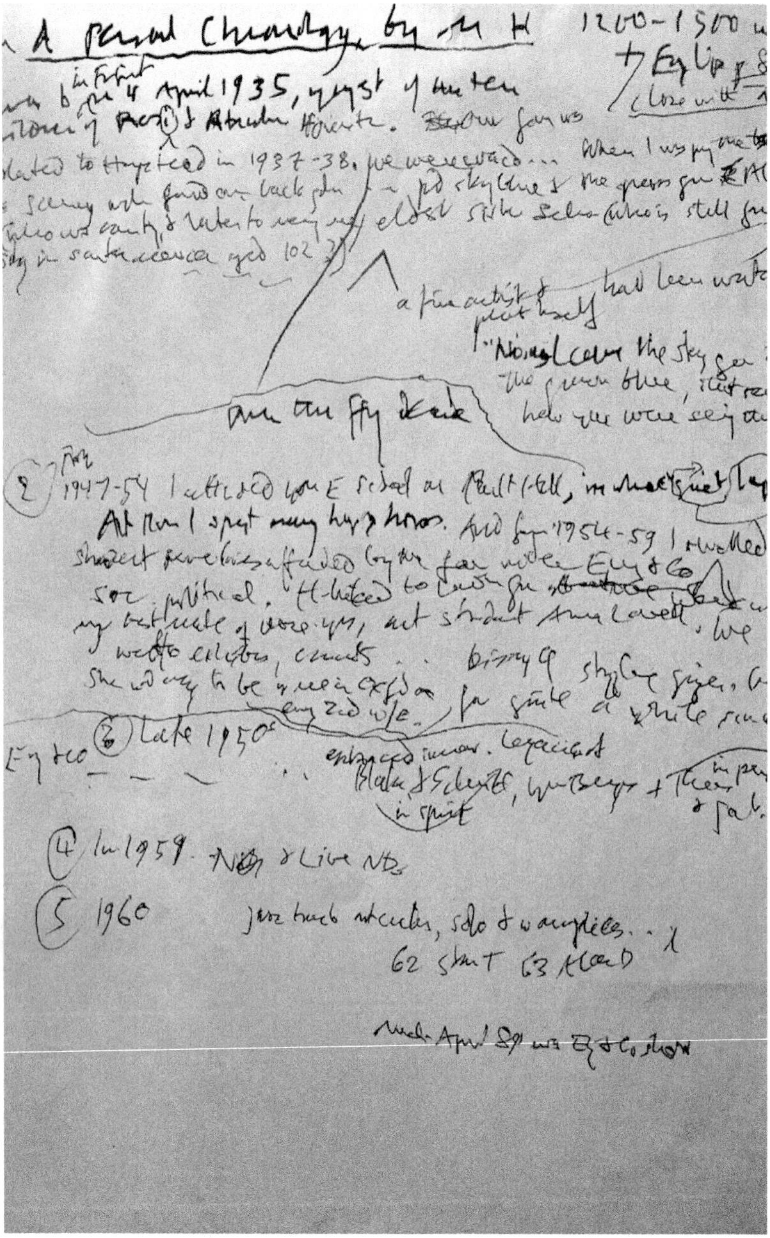
A Personal Chronology by M H
1200–1500
4 April 1935
1937–38
1947–54
1954–59
Late 1950s
In 1959
1960
62
63

MALCOLM RITCHIE

Excerpts from THE SHAPING OF AN OUTSIDER
The Search for Self in a Wounded Landscape

Chapter 7

straw raincoat in Hokusai print
smell it drying out still
over three centuries ago

A Cornish Art School

I now had nowhere to go but 'home', where as far as my father was concerned, I was persona non grata. In fact, I was informed by my mother that my father had actually "cut me off" – a term for disinheriting which carries the implication of castration. Since he had already executed this severing at every stage of my young life, there was nothing of an 'attachment' that could have been disconnected or broken.

My father had by this time become the commanding officer of an air-sea rescue squadron of helicopters, whose base was located in Cornwall. It was shortly after his taking up this post that he appears to have been beset by either delusions of grandeur, or the onset of a somewhat premature mid-life crisis. He purchased an Austin Princess. A long, black limousine furnished with an electrically operated glass screen which separated the driver – in anticipation of the driver being a chauffeur – from the passengers in the back. It was here, for the entertainment of passengers, that there was a cupboard which opened to reveal a cocktail cabinet. It was, I think, really a kind of 'Rolls Royce' built for the nouveau riche, but would appear to have been more commonly put into service as a hearse. However, as this sleek carriage glided and curtsied its way along tight Cornish lanes, rather than causing my sister and I to feel privileged or impressed by the manner of our transportation, we simply felt acutely embarrassed.

Also accompanying us on these stately excursions was a recently-acquired hound. Nina was a beautiful, benign, brindled, thoroughbred bull-mastiff bitch with an impressive pedigree, who, when she was in heat would occasionally escape and run around the district. Due to her well-developed jowls, she would foam at the mouth and terrify everyone who encountered her. She once appeared on the parade ground during a parade, causing all the ranks to scatter for the shelter of surrounding buildings.

Cornwall, situated in the farthest southwest reaches of Britain, was once an independent Celtic country with its own distinct culture and language. Unbeknown to me at the time, I had arrived in a part of the country that would become my adopted home for many years. I took a variety of jobs that included working for a short time in a pet shop, followed by work in a second-hand bookshop in Newquay, and then for a bus tour company. It was a time when Cornwall had again become a mecca for artists and writers, as it had been for many years previously. Its population also included a new phenomenon called 'beatniks' – hippie proto-types and the inheritors of the mantle of what had been known as 'bohemians', but whose philosophy and way of living had been imported from America.

Newquay and its surrounding countryside was a home to a group of this wild tribe, made up of an assortment of painters, musicians, poets and dreamers. Seeing these characters, amongst whom was the musician Wizz Jones, an acoustic guitarist, later to become well-known on the music scene, walking about the town and wandering the beaches with their long hair and beards, open-toe sandals and unkempt clothes was both a revelation and an inspiration to me. It suggested an antidote to the stifling and arid middleclass, bourgeois environment filled with its fears, false politeness, pale imitation of religion and its creed of materialism and 'security'.

I immediately began to continue what I had begun as a reaction to my life in the Air Force, to draw and paint badly and write unpromising poetry. I stuck a Franz Marc reproduction and a couple of Japanese prints up on my bedroom wall and felt as though I might be becoming someone else. I also began to self-consciously dress in what I imagined was a beatnik fashion: wearing two shirts at a time, one over the other, with a neckerchief or scarf tied loosely around my neck. My parents became increasingly paranoid about what our neighbours in the officers' quarters would think; a perennial concern. While my father assumed his worst fears had been visited upon him. I had gone 'queer' and finally succumbed to the emasculating paw of masturbation!

Endorsing his suspicion even further, I applied to the art school in Falmouth, where, on passing a simple drawing exam, I was accepted. At that time, the board of governors and visiting lecturers were drawn from the deep well of artists who had settled and worked in and around the St. Ives area: Peter Lanyon, Bernard Leach, Barbara Hepworth, Terry Frost, Bryan Winter and Patrick Heron among them.

The main heart and dynamo of Falmouth then, as it had been for centuries, was safe anchorage in the third deepest natural harbour in the world, with the docks employing the major part of the male working force. It was and remains, the first and last port of call in Britain, and was where the famous female spy Mata Hari was landed after her arrest in Spain, before being transported to London. It has its own microclimate which is wet and warm and Mediterranean in character.

When I arrived there in the late fifties, it still retained a nineteenth century atmosphere. Many of the houses including the railway station were still lit by gas lamps and heated by coal fires. The tug boats were all steam driven, and the crews would row out to them, singing the rhythm to their oars, and on a misty day, the harbour would take on the foggy appearance of a nineteenth century daguerreotype. Fishermen in their yards, would sing a cappella while mending their nets, and later in the evening before the pubs closed, decorate the night air of the darkened high street with their close harmonies, sweetened by alcohol.

My first lodgings, which I shared with one other student, was with a family called Scantlebury. Both the father and son worked in the docks. The son always referred to us as "the twisted", reflecting an oppositional tension between the students and the townsfolk which was to become more pronounced and polarised as we entered the sixties. The "twisted" coming to represent an even more extreme otherness and threat to the local "no-good-boyos", while also giving rise to a probably unacknowledged jealousy, with our apparent freedom and pretended disregard for convention, and regularly in the company of attractive young women.

The student I shared my room with was called Daniel; another disturbed young man who lived with his divorced mother, whom I later learned, was in the habit of regularly bringing home an assortment of different men. Dan was obsessed with James Dean, whose film Rebel Without a Cause – depicting a teenager's reaction to the suffocation of suburban life in 50s America – had recently been released and become in itself a catalyst or prompting for rebellion in many a middle-class youth on this side of the Atlantic. Dan produced slickly competent pencil portraits of Dean, and would spend hours late into the night, staring at himself from different angles in the mirror. It is possible he suffered the same problem of seeing himself as I had had myself, and was just making sure he was still there, or was at least as real to himself as James Dean was in his own head. Many years later, he was searched for by the police in connection with a murder which had taken place in a public lavatory.

After about a year, I moved my lodgings to The Manse overlooking Falmouth Bay and the harbour, in Trevethan Road. It was owned and run as a lodging house by Mrs Ellis, a retired cook who had saved her pennies. Mrs. Ellis was a ginger-haired, rotund woman with a retroussé, turned-up nose, and the florid complexion of a boiled ham, who resembled a combination of the characters in

Tenniel's illustration in Alice's Adventures in Wonderland of the cook and the Duchess who is nursing a baby pig, and the pig itself.

When I went for my interview and to see the room and house generally, I was shown into a back room next to the kitchen. While conversing with Mrs. Ellis, my attention was constantly distracted by the sight of a pile of old shoes burning in the fireplace, surmounted by a cock's head with an eye bubbling in its socket. This altogether strange apparition, like a vision issuing from the witches brew in Macbeth, immediately confirmed my opinion that this was the right place.

After agreeing on the rent and the rules of the house, I was about to leave, when Mrs. Ellis stopped me in the hallway, and looking up at me said, "I hope you don't mind me saying so, my dear, but you have the face of an angel." She was soon to revise this misapprehension, however, when coming to the realisation that if I did appear to have the "face of an angel", it was of a fallen angel! She was a year or so later, to detain me similarly in the hallway, but now furnished with this knowledge, say plaintively, "I don't mind what two bodies do with each other, my dear, but I wish you wouldn't do it in my front room!"

There was one old resident who became our bete noire. His name was, appropriately enough since the house overlooked the harbour, Mr. Seaward. He was a man of great misery, whose every physical movement was accompanied by a strange intermittent humming, as though to remind himself of the reality of his existence. Whenever I was up in the attic with a girlfriend, he would shout up the stairs, "He should be castrated! Castrated!"

Each Sunday morning for months, our sleep was interrupted by the Salvation Army playing their brass instruments in the road outside the house. Finally, my friend John Cutting and I began reacting like Jimmy Porter to the church bells in Osborne's Look Back in Anger. On several occasions we opened the skylight in the roof and shouted profanities at them to no avail. But one Sunday, John who had somehow acquired a starting pistol, opened the skylight, and calling their attention, fired the gun at them. We were never disturbed again. Having suffered myself at school from a starting pistol, I understood their reluctance to return.

Another permanent resident at the Manse, was a man with a lame leg called Jack, who always had an unlit pipe stuck in his mouth. He was unable to work and helped out around the house and garden as Mrs. Ellis's handyman. He kept an equally lame-and-named jackdaw in a cage outside the kitchen door, which we would occasionally feed surreptitiously with the leftovers from our meals.

Hanging on the back of the kitchen door, there was always a pair of Mrs. Ellis's marquee-sized knickers on which she would wipe her hands while cooking our meals, and often give her face a turn or two. At night, slugs would trespass on her rotting, wooden draining-boards, only to be dissolved into a frothing mass in the morning by Mrs. Ellis liberally sprinkling them with salt. And on the occasions that we would arrive late at night after she had gone to her bed, we would often find one of her several cats sleeping curled up in the breakfast frying pan. Another occasional sight on the top of her gas cooker was a saucepan of boiling water containing an alarm clock. She claimed that it was the only remedy for restarting them after they had stopped working.

It all reminds me now, of just how wonderful and poetic life was before the neurosis of 'health and safety', and a contaminating suburban ethos bearing its obsession with cleanliness and propriety set in like toxic weather over the land.

Chapter 10

"Plants remember a time when everything was interconnected in a holy synergy."

Heathcote Williams –
Manifestoes/Manifesten

A Transatlantic Visit

Sometime in the early sixties, I submitted an 'experimental' piece of writing to the Transatlantic Review. I did not really have much expectation it would be accepted. However, a short while later and much to my amazement, I received a letter saying they would very much like to publish it. Later, after having got to know the editor, Heathcote Williams, I considered there must have been a pulse, a bloom given off from my piece and carried on the schizoid rhythms of its text, which attracted him.

A few weeks later, one morning, there was a ring at the door of our flat above an antiques shop in Falmouth where I worked restoring furniture and keeping shop when the owner was away. I opened the door to a man of about my own age, attired in a brown pin-striped suit with flared trousers and a head of electrically excited hair, who introduced himself, appropriately mimicking a transatlantic accent, "Hi, I'm Heathcote Williams from the Transatlantic Review".

I was immediately impressed, and we quickly repaired to the Ship and Castle, a pub in the middle of town known locally as the "Shit and Arsehole". It must have been the only pub in Cornwall, and possibly Britain in those days, to have a transvestite behind the bar. It was the pub most frequented by the local queer community, whores and sailors, and members of the Cornish Republican Army, who were at the time planning, at least in their imaginations, to blow up the newly-built road bridge across the Tamar River that separated Cornwall from England. Years later, I came to appreciate exactly how it was the right ambience for our initial introduction.

At this time, Heathcote was restricted to drinking tonic water and lemon, since he had only recently been cured of alcoholism by the parapsychologist Joan Grant. She and her husband, psychiatrist Denys Kelsey had regressed him, under hypnosis, beyond the womb to a past-life memory of being tortured during the Spanish Inquisition. He apparently re-experienced having his tongue cut out. According to Heathcote, they had difficulty counting him back to the present, and once they had succeeded, he immediately drank seven carafes of water. The cause of his alcoholism was attributed to the deeply repressed memory of this trauma, and the conditioned need to assuage the pain of his past-life glossectomy, by excessive drinking – the tongue, of course, being an essential organ for any actor or performer of poetry, both of which he was.

Our meeting was so natural and strangely familiar that it was almost as though we too were reconnecting from some past life, ourselves. This first meeting was the overture to what from that moment on became a lifelong, karmic friendship; an introduction to the person who, incrementally, I came to feel was my spirit-brother. He was the one being, apart from my present wife, Masako, I have felt closest to in my life, as though we may have been evicted from the same womb. As it turned out, his "eviction" was far more successful than mine, and he was in possession of the greater gifts. He once told me that his wife, Diana, had said that I was his alter ego.

We were both damaged people, born in war and surrounded by fearful adults, while each of us carried a father problem that had us initially, as well-yoked sons, following in our fathers' footsteps – Heathcote into Law, and as described, me into the Royal Air Force. It is the suffering and awareness of our damage that causes many of us to be creative, as some kind of corrective response – an attempt to make a wholeness in outer forms that is denied within.

Heathcote had been schooled in the crucible of the British Establishment at Eton, and as in Lindsay Anderson's film If, he soon contracted an aversion to its environment and spent the rest of his life taking pot-shots at it from its roof. While he was out in the world, changing his skin; moving and shaking, and sloughing off his class allegiances; becoming streetwise and very much the urban pirate/provocateur, and enfin terrible; I was from a Scottish boarding school in the wilds of the borderlands of Alba, followed by several English grammar schools; generally adrift without keel or sail, and reclusive by nature. I was already losing interest in Western culture and in the societies it spawns.

Heathcote, while rejecting the British Establishment, remained very much within a particular English tradition of radical thought and sensibility as expressed and evidenced in most everything he wrote, and in his socio-political activism, charged with a healthy, native anarchic spirit. Even as an 'outsider', he was well-embedded within his Western/English cultural milieu. I, by contrast, was looking East.

He had that kind of charismatic, psycho-gravitational field about him that immediately drew you to him. He was puckish, mercurial, with an air of the puer aerternus (eternal youth). He was a Peter Pan who seemed endlessly successful in eluding the Crocodile of Time, while wielding his pen. He was ever the actor, a performer who needed an audience. One afternoon, many years into our friendship, when he was depressed after the breakdown of a relationship following the publication of his long prose poem, Whale Nation, he turned to me and said, "You know Malcolm, I only feel real when I'm being someone else". This reminded me of Oscar Wilde saying, "I love acting. It's so much more real than life." Heathcote once told me that he had slept in the very room in the hotel in France where Wilde had died. "They hadn't changed the wallpaper," he said, referring to Wilde's reaction on first entering the room, and declaring, "This wallpaper is terrible, one of us must go!"

I very quickly found myself, as I am sure did many others, willingly becoming his servant, a co-conspirator, a runner, a fetcher, a supplier, a brother pirate, a searcher, re-searcher, and sometimes spy. I remember many occasions when he would ask me to keep an eye open for something or other, or actively hunt something down. On one occasion he had executed a drawing of William Burroughs – which later became the cover of an issue of the Transatlantic Review – and asked me what kind of frame I thought would suit it. It happened that the previous week I had seen a python skin in a junkshop window, so I readily purchased it for the purpose. On another occasion, in these pre-Internet days, when he was writing a script for a film based on the infamous siege of Sidney Street, he asked me if I could track down a book describing the incident in which Winston Churchill, as Home Secretary, prevented the fire brigade gaining access to the street where a house in which a number of anarchists had sought refuge, had caught fire, resulting in all of the occupants perishing, apart from one who escaped. A man with the soubriquet Peter the Painter. I found a copy in a second-hand bookshop.

It was shortly after meeting Heathcote, and with little or no knowledge of his life, I became aware of the performer in him. One late night in my kitchen, he was telling me a story while acting out the various characters involved. I was standing with my back to a glass door which led into the garden. Suddenly, I became aware that he was not actually looking at me, but was watching himself in the reflective surface of the glass. He was a genius at turning his later works into presentations he wrote, designed, produced, often performed, and promoted. While always waiting in the wings of his main roles as poet, playwright, and writer, Heathcote was a magician and lifetime member of The Magic Circle, fire-eater, political/social activist, actor, painter, song writer, inventor and more. A protean being – a societal shaman.

The first invention of his that I became aware of, was a mirror in which you always appeared beautiful: a "Mirror, mirror on the wall…" kind of mirror. I forget exactly how it was constructed, but there were several layers of glass, and when you looked into it, there was a kind of oceanic blue-green halo around your countenance. One of his inventions, many years later, was a humane bug trapper, for which he had drawn an elaborate design and promotional material. He asked my partner, Masako, if she could write a description and instructions in Japanese with the idea of opening up a Far East market for it. He had already produced the prototype, but I had not the heart to tell him that there had been several similar models on the market for a number of years.

Heathcote stayed at least one night on that first visit, at a time when he was about to have his brilliant book The Speakers, published. He came to stay thereafter on several occasions while I was in Cornwall, often when he was also visiting his old friend from Eton, Peregrine Eliot, 10th Earl of St. Germans, at Port Eliot, close to the Tamar River.

At that time, still in his early twenties, he seemed impressed and energised by the world of fame. My later perception was he lived in the tension between the poles of two seemingly oppositional desires; wanting to be a star while wishing to be an anonymous recluse – ironically managing to successfully conflate both of these positions during old age and illness. He impressed me with the huge and diverse network of people he knew. It ranged from well-known actors, politicians, and members of the aristocracy, to criminals, road-sweepers, writers, artists, and political activists. And while having known many artists, writers, poets and other creatives, I have never met anyone with such creative consistency and stamina as Heathcote. Each moment; each sound, sight, thought, over-hearing, idea and circumstance could be utilized and transformed into verses of his life-song.

He once told me that after he had dropped out of Oxford, and was fraternizing with the speakers in Hyde Park – about whom he later wrote The Speakers referred to above – he got into a terrible argument with his father, "in the library", when his father called him "a useless bum", provoking an actual physical fight between them. Shortly afterwards, his father had died, and Heathcote confided to me that he often worried he might have killed him. I have occasionally wondered if it was Oedipal energy that might have driven him to continually try to prove himself not “a bum” to the ghost of a father he feared he may have killed. But this is only conjecture and may well have nothing to do with the fecundity of Heathcote’s extraordinary polymathic gifts.

Chapter 11

"...it is an odd world in which it takes a crime to get people to look at a Rembrandt."

Daily Telegraph November 5th 1965

The Rembrandt Heist

One of Heathcote's most memorable visits to Cornwall during our early friendship, led to our stealing a Rembrandt drawing from Truro Museum and Art Gallery. He was terrified during his lifetime, that this story would be made public even after the Statute of Limitations had long expired, because he did not want his "enemies" to get hold of it.

While waiting for a train to Falmouth to visit me, Heathcote had stopped in the museum and art gallery in Truro and noticed a drawing by Rembrandt had been hung with another framed drawing beneath it. The drawing in question – wrongly described later in newspaper reports – depicted a man attired for bed in nightgown and cap and holding a candlestick, with his wife similarly attired in the background. He relayed this information to me, while we went into town to meet up with a mutual friend Barry, who lived in Penryn, a short distance up the Penryn River from Falmouth. The three of us decided to take the ferry across to the village of Flushing, on the opposite side from Falmouth. There, in a field at the end of the village, while smoking a couple of joints, and sharing the story with Barry, a plan began to hatch itself to steal the drawing. Since having already been kicked out of the Air Force, and then removed from art school, it simply seemed to me like something already inked-in on my CV without need for either reason or motive.

As the idea spun into its own orbit, it began to develop a gravitational attraction for us. Heathcote volunteered that he knew of a fence in Paris who might be able to deal with the drawing. His own part in the escapade was to guard the stairs while Barry executed the deed, removing the drawing from the wall and secreting it in a briefcase. For my part, I was to detain all the staff in the office with my collection of Romano-British pottery sherds, and from where I would have a good view of the stairs through a window in the office door.

However, things did not seem to go so well, as my co-conspirators kept returning to the ground floor and signalling that I should remain in the office. This occurred three times until they finally signalled success, by which time I had run out of questions and was desperately searching for another subject of enquiry.

We had arranged to meet at the bus station and return to Falmouth together, but by the time the bus driver had started the engine, I remained the only passenger on the top deck. So convinced was I that they had been caught, that, charged with anxiety, I alighted from the bus at Penryn and walked the remaining distance into Falmouth across fields. Once home, I waited nervously. About three hours later, Barry turned up in an agitated state and asked me if I would hide his jacket and sweater for him, as he was afraid they might identify him. It was then that I realised, that of the three of us, I was most likely the only one who actually risked being identified.

Apparently, the frame had proved too large for the briefcase. They had had to go out and buy a bag from the stationers WH Smiths, which had again proved too small, until finally, in the manner of folk-and-fairy tales, the third proved just right. They had then descended into the crypt of Truro Cathedral and hidden the frame, a pair of gloves, and a pair of pliers in a chest used for the storage of surplices and other ritual paraphernalia. Heathcote had placed the drawing in an envelope and posted it off to the office of the Transatlantic Review with "MS." scrawled on it, after which, according to Barry, he boarded a train for Paddington in an agitated state of paranoia.

There was silence for a couple of weeks, until I received a postcard from Heathcote bearing the first couple of lines from Louis MacNiece's Bagpipe Music, which goes, "It's no good the merrygoround/It's no good the rickshaw…" letting me know that he had not been able to off-load the drawing. In the meantime, a policeman had come into the shop with the shocking news that a valuable Rembrandt drawing had been stolen from Truro Museum and Art Gallery, and that if anything suspicious should be offered to us for sale, would we contact them. I received this news with laudable surprise and interest.

A few days later, my boss's newspaper, The Daily Telegraph carried a report of the theft in which, for me, the final paragraph proved vindication, and which I sent to Heathcote. It suggested that "…it is an odd world in which it takes a crime to get people to look at a Rembrandt." One newspaper, a week or so later, reported that the drawing had turned up at the National Gallery bearing the legend on its back: CELTIC PROTEST FOR HOME RULE! Concluding that it was "…obviously the work of cranks."

SAIRA VIOLA:

HORIZONTAL VERTICAL

A low swung smile on her heart shaped face. Topless in bordello - red panties. Her left leg slung at a ninety-degree angle across a black scrunched cocktail dress. Her right leg straddled the arm of an easy- fit budget sofa upholstered in an aggressive shade of convict orange. On the floor beside her an open tub of vaginal jelly three fingers of blow and a dinky gold-plated cocaine spoon. It was noon. The sun vomiting diluted rays of insipid light into the room. A slit of dust on the coffee table and a shit- strewn kitty litter box sat by the back wall. It stunk of broken promises. Kiki Loveheart aka Mizz WhipKink aka Maddie Summers aka Sweet Cheeks 69 eking out a piece meal existence as intermittently: daytime nurse - afternoon phone sex operator - nighttime glamour escort and weekend stripper. Forced to juggle four jobs just to live in a cramped foul- smelling roach -ridden walk up. She Stared ruefully at her purple jazz- berry mirrored Jimmy Choo's. She felt like a Penthouse pin up in those heels. They elongated her calf muscles popped her pelvis and kinked her hips. Strutting the sidewalk never felt so good. Kiki blinked- yawned and slowly threw the remnants of the dawn away in brown paper bag. She got up. Barefoot. Tip-toed to the refrigerator and took out a cold bottle of fizzy mineral water then rolled it against her forehead.

'Ahh.'
'Keeeeeki?'

A goopy taffy-laced little voice. It could have belonged to a whiny third grader, but it belonged to Michael Wiesel. A squiffy-eyed fatso who also happened to be a nasty sex perv, serial fraudster and celebrity TV Judge. Presiding over his own prime time panties and garters litigation series where ordinary people would take their problems to the peoples' court. Miserable little suburban dramas. Scripted for mass consumption. Of course, it was a ratings winner and Wiesel wore his success like an electric lit billboard. His patterned argyle socks vintage Rolex, silk -satin tux and two-ply cotton designer shirt screamed smug money. But his ageing blond-comb over pomaded across his jutting forehead - swollen butt -gut and peeling pink skin humbled him on occasions especially at funerals country clubs and IRS meetings.

'Keeeeeki. C'meer. I want chou to freshen up. Put on a dress or somethin' pretty. Clean yaw self-up, bitch. Syphilitic ghetto slut! You got no class.'

He threw a couple of c notes on the floor flashing his platinum-circled pinkie. His loose-lipped flappy pig mouth slapping her butt with yet another slew of insults: 'You need a tan – lose a few pounds – I like your hair straight - classy chicks wear perfume - get bigger tits…'

Twenty-eight years old and still listening to fruitless fuck balls who reminded her that she was just a split second vignette in THE BIG PICTURE. She switched her gaze between a moldy slice of Kraft deli-deluxe and Wiesel's spreading bald spot. Swirling her tongue around her index finger. She winked.

'Got a better idea.'
'Yeah?'
'Hmmmm. Why don't I text Nahhhtashhha ? And we mix it up.'
Natashaar: Twentyish. Nouveau redhead. Faux-Russian accent big bazookas, shapely ass, creamy lips. Sweeter than Nutella, a PHD student and Kiki's bestie. The pair of them responsible for a rash of tricks that would make even the hardest hustler blush.

'Whaddya have in mind?'
'Wait and see.'
'Do it.'
'Okayyyyy. Make yourself more comfortable. Take off your pants.'

Kiki grabbed her phone from the dresser. Natasha would be there in a few minutes. Wiesel caught between the bastard of time and

his own carnal greed. Pacing the floor like a red wattled hog he belched 'Hurry up.'
'She won't be long. Relax. Sit down. C'mon.'

She patted the seat with a fiendish glint in her eye. Then slid on thigh-high velvet boots and a black leather string bikini. Wiesel's creeper eye rested on her downy v-shape mound that peeped through the slit of her gusset. She muttered: 'I'm now officially at Ground zero. Knee deep in the butt end of the sex trade. Puny limp dick with big dick complex. Today I'm jumping off that pyramid ..'

'Whaddaya say. Speak up?'
'I said you know you make me so hot for it.'

The creases on Wiesel's face lined with dust and type 2 diabetic sweat. Everything Kiki did to make things better slam-jammed into nothing and now here she was star of her own dime -store crime story. Her mind somersaulting at freeway speed: Cancer-table sex-a black swan-yogi-tea homilies-dead-sister cancer be-yourself shaman-mantras-truck stop suicides-cancer blue-rubber covered-asses booby-trapped commitment-rib eye steak pus-filled promises -Je Je Spa-Happy Ending Massage Kung Fu nuns Himalayas auto-erotic strangulation.

Squatting on a throne of debt, Kiki was tired of sleazo tricksters. Tired of renting herself out to small-souled roly-poly hardballs. Tired of one bowl -easy mac frozen dinners- three-minute hustles with teenage dopers and cheapo plastic heart break. Her brain backed up with years of toxic yesterdays. Ever since her only sister had succumbed to cancer. She felt trapped like a fly in vinegar. She wanted out. Wiesel. He was the catalyst. Sprawled there on her green plastic lawn chair. Balancing papers on his balloon shaped stomach he tapped his foot to an invisible beat. Kiki stiffened. The double thump of her heart an erratic jump a second too fast. She had a driving primal urge to glass Wiesel in the neck. Slowly she played out every move in the dungeon of her mind. Psych out!

It wasn't the most original way to kill someone but it was definitely doable. It made her body tingle. She knew that Wiesel kept at least 10 grand in his grab bag. A pre-packed emergency kit stocked with doomsday end of the world shit. Wiesel carried it everywhere he went, bragging to anyone who'd listen that he was ready for Armageddon. It was the perfect get away bag. Ideal for two huzzies on the lam. Kiki's murder plan simmered. Something gross and a little immoral was about to happen.

'Ding dong.'
'That'll be Natassha.'

Kiki buzzed her up. Wiesel moistened his mouth and schlepped to the bed huffing his fairy tale sex romp through pepto bismol coughs.

Natasha bounced into view. A red pigtailed elfin faced kiss of light. 'Well, helllllooooo! How ya doing?' With her soft buttery face big, bruised lips and Betty Boop eyes she was ready to tease. Trussed up in a plaid schoolgirl mini and white shirt with a striped tie dangling around her waist, she cupped Kiki's face in her hands and gave her a long wet kiss.

Wiesel unbuttoned his shirt, revealing an expanse of silver and brown gorilla chest hair and a thatch of white fuzz that sprung from the nape of his neck. He stank of onions and tuxedoed fraud 'You know what I love about your type?' He tracked the curves of Kiki's thighs. Natasha pulled away grinning her way to the foot of the bed.

'Our type?'
'Yeah, pussy princesses.' Kiki's eyes narrowed.
'What?'
Ignoring the sarcastic inflexion in her voice. Wiesel sucked in his teeth.

'You understand that sex is just a business. I don't have to think too hard. I fuck you. Pay you. You're: MINE.'

His mildew eyes clung to her ass. She had to dig her nails in her palms to stop herself from puking in his lap. In a bittersweet tone part Marilyn Monroe part Morticia Adams she whispered:
'Let's try something new.'

A dangerous smile caressed her lips. Together they cuffed Wiesel to the bed. Kiki placed a blindfold on his eyes.

'C'mon, let's get on with it.' He growled.

Kiki and Natasha shared a knowing wink. Natasha jiggled her hips in Wiesel's face, toying with him while Kiki got busy.

'You think you know our type? Think again!'
'Aaaaaaaargh!'

She gagged him with a pair of sheer stockings. Deaf to his protestations. The gentle curve of her mouth promised more pain. Natasha bound his ankles with bondage tape kinky leather restraints. Kiki steamed:

'It's you and your type. You're the limp dick asshole who's got your greedy cheating hands all over the city. Everybody knows you're as crooked as hell. We're the only ones hurting.'

Kiki marched into the kitchenette. Smashed the water bottle against the wall and stomped back to the bedroom. Ignoring the squeaky yelps and blood spittle dribbling down Wiesel's chin. He thrashed around like a bottom -trawled fish gasping for air. Kiki gripped the base of the bottle jabbed it into his neck and sliced open his throat. She hit both carotid arteries and his jugular. Blood rhymes splattered the sheets. A symphony of choking strawberries. Warm. Red mulch.

They racked up the balance of the coke Kiki armed with the grab bag. 'C'mon let's get outta here.'

A few moments of thin silence. Kiki's voice strangely alien eaten by the shadows in the room:

'Ghetto sluts like me. Always end up vertical not horizontal.'

PAYDAY

Mark Schneider. Law school dropout. Part-time drunk. Serial masturbator. High-functioning meth addict. Sex bot devotee. Ex-husband, and one of LAPD's finest.

Early morning: Parked outside Baby Blues in an unmarked grey Chrysler 300, still code 3 equipped. His white shirt unbuttoned, revealing a full pecan tinted rug. Cuff sleeves turned back. His black pants were unzipped, and his cock poked out of striped jockeys. Schneider had a sock missing and a solitary long frizzy white hair dangled from his left nostril. Checking his face in the rear-view mirror, he yanked the hair out. 'Son of a bitch. You still got it.' He ran the tips of his fingers down the right side of his face. A face, chequered with mistakes, money fights, and unreported murder.

Schneider smoothed his shirt down, zipped up, and rummaged around in the back seat. Sifting through paper coffee cups, potato chip packets, a half-drunk bottle of Jameson, and a dozen grease spotted Five Guys burger bags, he grabbed his anti-perspirant stick. Twist. Click. He slicked both armpits. Then he spied a little mouthful of sunlight. A sparkly faced cutie Marla Cortez skipped right in front of him. She had just finished her shift at the Golden Banana and was on her way home. Marla had to take care of her mom who had a heart condition and her little brother Oscar.
She flung off her denim jacket revealing a sea green tube top and hiked up her skirt allowing the youthful rush of summer heat, to embrace her as she wheeled her hips around. Her pink-string tanga on show. High High High. Smiling honkers on display. She was all taste as she hop-scotched towards the patrol car, caterwauling , tuneless karaoke style rhymes, with a Kool Aid cup in her hand. Her apple shaped ass winking. Jiggle. Jiggle Jiggle. Like the soft round sound of a Tenor trombone.

Schneider's smutty eye preyed on Marla's intoxicating euphoria. 'Fresh.'

He leant back in his seat, slid his hand down to his leg, and winced as he lifted the hem of his pants. A dime sized hole in the middle of his right calf dripped blood. He blotted it dry with a stained paper towel and tossed it in the back seat.

'Small fish are easy prey', he muttered. 'Pat and frisk. Every curve. Inside thigh and sugar walls.' He opened the car door using the Dutch Reach technique, so he could easily spot any on coming distractions, or potential witnesses. 'Excuse me Miss.'

Marla was in her own kookookechoo bubble. A boho suede purse hung from her neck. 'Yeeeeeh.'
'Could you please step this way?'
'Er…What for?'
'Coz I asked you to.'

Marla sniffed.

'You got no right to ask me anything Officer. I'm not doing anything wrong. Lemme pass please.'
Schneider looked at her like a captive animal. 'You ain't shit baby. You ain't nuthin and you ain't going nowhere.'
'But I've done nuthing wrong.'

Schneider 's power was sewn up tight in the furrows of his face. Marla tried to side step away, but Schneider blocked her path with his leg and showed off his gun tucked in his waistband.

'Sir. Please. Just let me through.'
'No. Fucking. Way.'

Marla spat on the ground. 'What the fuck is going on.'
Under her breath she hissed 'Bbbbbbastard!'
'Whooooa. Eassseee tiger.' Without blinking, Schneider pinned her arms behind her back and used his left hand to control her. Within seconds, she was cuffed. He forced her to stand, against the car legs apart, and placed his big meaty fingers around her waist.

After patting her down, he groped her left butt cheek. 'You got your ID?'

Marla flinched.
Then he groped her right butt cheek.

Her eye lashes instinctively quivered 'D...Don't touch me!'
'Cool it honey. You're slurring your words, and there's that crazy eye twitch. You reek of weed and pcp. And you're in a lot of trouble. It doesn't look good for you. Not at all. No mam. Thing is liddle lady, I'm entitled to touch. Anywhere I want. Cos, I got a feelin' you're concealin'. And your freaky -deaky necked shit makes me think you're under the influence of a drug or controlled substance. But I'm a nice guy. I'm thinkin' you and me can work somethin' out.' He caught the warmth of her body as he stood behind her with his cock pressed hard against her ass and slipped his fingers into the back of her panties. 'You know what I want.'
Marla opened her mouth as wide as she could her tonsils trying to spread the injustice. 'Arrrrrrrrrrrrggghhh!'

Schneider lunged deeper and squeezed her snatch. 'One more word and I'll fuck the shit right out of you.'

Marla tossed her head back and mule-kicked him in the shin.
He stumbled, picked himself up and untied the purse from her neck. 'Now what we got here? Some kind o' prairie hippie shit?'
Inside her purse, Marla had her driver's license, cell phone, a tiny tube of cherry lip balm an EBT card, and some foil wraps.
Schneider held the purse under his right arm walked her to the other side of the car then placed her headfirst into the front passenger seat. He sat on the driver's side and pretended to run her intel through his police laptop. 'We got a real messy situation. Clearly, you're under the influence of some kinda drug probably some alkhi–hol too. Completely outta of control in a public place. So, you're a danger to yourself and everyone around you.'
He held up the foil wraps. 'And what we got here? Some leftovers? A little angel dust. Krissst.'

Schneider's face grew uglier. 'Girl you're fucked! Well, what's it gonna be big Jim and the twins or a trip to the precinct and county lock up? Get down girl. C'mon. Get down.'

A string of tears beaded Marla's eyes 'You wa...want mmme t' suck yoooo off th… then y yyou let ...me go?'
'That's right.'
'Bbbbbbbastard!'
'I saw the EBT card. Dunno why they bother with that shit. You can't buy jack. No vitamins, no beer, and no cigarettes. So, what the fuck's it good for? If you accept my offer, at least you'll be getting a dose of good ol' American protein. Just you and me. It's a very generous offer.'

Marla clawed her own hands. A form of self-protest. 'Wh..what kind of fucked up po- po are you anyway?'
'The real kind. Dirty. Reliable. Now we got a deal or what?'
Schneider unzipped his pants.
'Now give it a long, slow suck Lollipop style…'
Schneider forced her head down. One hand gripped the back of her neck. Pastel ribbons of vomit began to build in her glottis. Schneider's 45 calibre Kimber Classic was aimed at her the whole time.

Marla felt as if her tongue was buried in white America, as if she had no control of her own body. Terror. She wanted to run. Run from his blistered thumbs and his sickly cologne. But one look at his malign little eyes and she hung on, like a trapped bird feeding her wounds into a deadly snake. When it was over, she remained perfectly still for a while, staring out of the window at a singing wave of blue sky.

Schneider dropped her off at a vacant parking lot near Family Dollar minimart. She sat on the curb and threw up. A five-minute technicolour barfing opera. All her dreams, missed opportunities, and nightmares splattered to the ground.

Schneider adjusted his pants and drove away, spanking the tarmac at speed. Pounding on the steering wheel, he screeched the lyrics to AC DC's Highway to Hell: 'No stop signs... no one's gonna slow me down.' In the cavities of his mind, Schneider believed he was a renegade, reacting against a system he'd stopped believing in long ago. To everyone else he was a lyin' dealin' snortin' stealin' crooked cop. The god of the unflushed crapper feasting on fresh blood.

THREE WEEKS LATER in Brodies Food Mart Marla watched as Schneider punched open the cash register and jammed his pockets with a stack of bills. The owner simply shrugged and turned away. Marla had been marking time: At the Rape Crisis center in West Hollywood. At the Free clinic for contact dermatitis. At the unemployment office. At Danny G's pawn shop hocking her sick mother's wedding ring so the family could eat. They were being squeezed left and right centre for car payments, credit card bills, and back rent but all she could think of was the greying stink of a dead white fish. She followed Schneider out of the door and hovered in a side street all the while fingering her small silver Milagro she carried around for luck and her newly acquired pocketknife. *You look like a big fat sweaty pig standing there waiting ...just waiting for the slaughter.* Schneider whistled at a petite strawberry-blonde wearing a tight lavender sweater over black jeggings and long black boots. She glanced at him nervously and hurried away. Schnieder was about to say something when suddenly out of the shadows two beef heads covered by ski masks fired three shots into the air:

BAM! BAM! BAM!

They raced towards a blacked-out Lincoln pushing past a phalanx of party goers waving their hands in the air. The driver in the Lincoln spun around and caught Schneider reaching for his gun, radioing for help. He jammed the brakes calmly pulled out a 38 caliber from the glove box and shot him straight through the window. Schneider arched over. His legs splintered and he took the full fall on the rump of his ass. Screams! A swash of blood and a welling crowd.

Schneider screeched 'I'm hit Jesus I'm hit.'

Squad cars and an ambulance arrived a few minutes later.
Marla edged her way through the rabble and stared at a sputtering red neon sign above her. PAYDAY.

CALLING LEO

Chi Chi was a petty dope dealer full-time fraudster and occasional paralegal. She had frittered away all of her meagre inheritance on footwear and frivolous froth like French designer jeans and lacy bedroom panties. Karl used to say she was a "poster pinup for the bourgeoisie." They broke up when she sold his flamenco guitar on e- bay and she fucked his best friend in the Café Rouge parking lot. She told him while they were watching a Netflix miniseries on sociopaths. She remembered his big sad eyes like two accusing dollar signs.

Midnight at Klub 7: Chi Chi tried to block a platoon of dark thoughts from clouding her mind as she double stepped her way to the bar and sat down next to a flirty old buzzard with a sexy gold tooth and a sunny laugh. She slipped off her jacket and struck a voguish pose. Hot Americano legs stole the limelight.

'Can I get you a drink?'

'Why thank you very much …'

'You can call me Bob.'

His voice reminded her of scratchy nettles.

'I'll have a rum and coke Bob.'

The barkeep sailed in from nowhere topped up Bob's glass and set hers on the counter. Chi Chi spied the hands of opportunity crawl through the twinkle of Bob's eyes.

'You're sneaky. You look like trouble with a capital T.'

She threw her head back and laughed and it was like uncorking a bottle of champagne.

'All my friends call me Chi Chi.'

Bob chuckled. 'You really know how to bust those moves. I'm like a constipated racoon out there.'

'Ah there's nothing to it you just jiggle and jive. Somehow it all comes together.'

Two whiskey bombed hours later Chi Chi slunk into Bob's exclusive beach hideaway. And when she stripped off, they became two frolicking waves in the ocean of the night.

Around 3:00 a.m. Chi Chi woke up. She could smell the drift of Johnnie Walker on Bob's grizzled face. She looked around in wonder. It was like a show house. Straight out of Harper's Bazaar. Her silent smile spread into a grin. She stared at Bob and his curbstone skin all gray and scaly like a map of unfinished endings.

There were all the signs of a big-ticket life but as she tiptoed around, she knew something was off. She couldn't decide if the chemi-trails in her brain were playing cheap tricks on her or if she'd really heard her mother's voice. Why?

She dug her nails deep into her palms to stop herself from crying.

'Mamma? Mamma? Where are you?'

Suddenly she felt a cold rush of air. Her nipples hardened. She crept back to bed and laid back down next to Bob. His throat hummed as he turned his body towards her. A sweaty tangle of strangeness and comfort.

She slept until noon. There was a little post it sticker on the dresser it read: Help yourself to champagne and eggs Bob xo. She hopped out of bed and floated into the kitchen. A vulgar smack of culinary porn. Big beamed ceilings and the ubiquitous stand-alone island. The refrigerator, a sleek stainless armoire of greedy decadence ate up two thirds of the room. Slowly she opened the door. Apart from all the crushed ice and luxe gourmet fare she spied a delicate black box pitted with air holes sitting on the middle shelf. She picked it up and turned it over. Hmm. I wonder. Probably a fancy schmancy block of cheese or maybe something a little more exotic.

She held it close to her ear and listened. It sounded like the chatter of old men praying; A spiritual mantra of some kind. Ya be Yae. Ya be Yae. A wave of disorientation and a scattering of stinging light. Chi Chi dropped the box terrified and on impulse scrambled for the door. She had a tight dry feeling in her throat. Her eyes dimmed and the last thing she saw was a fury of red ants dancing around her ankles as she collapsed onto the cold terracotta tiles.

When she finally woke up a slap of green neon enveloped her. It covered the walls, the ceiling and the barrel of a Glock 43 inches away from her head. She gulped and stole a breath. This can't be real …In her mind she rationalised a neo Lynchian film of distraction. Soon the three-foot talking blue haired munchkins would bounce into view and she could catch up on some well needed sleep. But instead, she was confronted with the lurid shadow of a woman. Her face hidden by a creepy theatre mask with the eyes and mouth hollowed out. One side tragedy the other comedy.

'Chi Chi. Even that name sounds fake. Like a cutesy liddle Pomeranian or one of those tacky Gangnam style cocktails. You know with a paper umbrella sticking out the top. Either way, it's so …You.' There was something eerily familiar about that greying voice. A voice sharpened with hate and Pepto bismol.

'This is a beautiful place eh Chi Chi?'

She nodded and tried to squint away all the sickly green.

'I don't understand I …Who ...?'

The woman laughed through her mask.

'You were always trying to be niceeee. So nice.'

Chi Chi felt the panic rise in her chest; Something ugly was about to happen she could feel it.
'Please. I ... Where's Bob?'
'Fuck Bob. You know what this is? A reckoning for all the nasty shit ...'

The woman slithered closer and laid her gloved palm across Chi Chi's cheek. 'I don't blame Bob sweetie. I blame you.' Chi Chi flinched and tried to back away, but she was hemmed in from all sides. Could that be Bob's wife or ...

There was a brief queasy silence.

'Who are you, what do you want from me?'
'Now that's a start. That's what I expect from a wannabe lawyer.'

The woman slipped off her mask with theatrical panache. 'You remember me don't you?'

Her face was a complex trail of unhappy yesterdays. Chi Chi could see all the misery of the world caged in that face. She tried to place her but all she could think of was Swedish fish and milk balls. Her stomach grumbled as she let out a short sigh.

'Why d'ya do it?'
A different piece of her said:
'Because I like drinking expensive champagne glamming it up with celebrities and partying with rich dudes. Because I hate slurping through the fringes of life on dime store cookies plastic plated chicken and top Ramen.'

The woman grinned and revealed a mushy purple gum line. 'You left me with nothing. So here I am working as a maid for Bob I get just enough to keep my Fico score alive and a stack of pancakes at Dennys every Friday.'

A tea-coloured wheeze landed on Chi Chi's thigh. 'I clean his toilet I wash his socks and mop cat piss from his floors because you stole from me.

Chi Chi flashed back to a sunny day in June. Elizabeth Rawlins a sixty-five-year-old widow had walked into the office and trusted her with every penny she had. And now a year ago to the day Chi Chi aka Cameron Bell sat face to face with her conscience.

Mrs. Rawlins had a surprisingly steady hand, but her voice was shaky.

'Why? You forged the deeds to my house you took it from me, and they burnt it to the ground.' She paused.

'Leo was inside.'

Chi Chi's lips tightened, and a look of panic engulfed her face. Mrs. Rawlins started to sob. 'Leo was more than just a cat. He was family. My best friend.'

Chi Chi sighed with relief.

She didn't think the old woman would do it, couldn't believe she was capable of pulling the trigger but that weird light in Mrs Rawlins eyes unsettled her. All she could see was a comet of mistakes if she didn't act fast. A three second pause. Chi Chi screeched and jumped towards her. Mrs. Rawlins toppled backwards and dropped the gun. Chi Chi made a scramble for the stairs but tripped on the third one. Mrs Rawlins limped forward grabbed her ankles and tried to drag her back. 'I'm gonna use every last breath ...'

Chi Chi kicked her away crawled to the top of the stairs, unbolted the front door, and ran...

Baja Mexico

Chi Chi sat alone sipping a Mai Tai cocktail watching the ruby crown of the sun sink beneath restless skies, when a stray tabby climbed into her lap. At first demure and coy she rubbed her head against Chi Chi's thigh. Then with a snooty hiss suddenly sprung round and swiped her left cheek with her wet paw. A scratch of red. The seams of Chi Chi's mouth slanted down as she tried to push it away. Too late! It sunk its' claws deep into the side of her face ripping open the corner of her left eye. Milky globs of red pus oozed to the bottom of her chin. Chi Chi let out a long piercing scream like a fire whistle.

'Help me! Somebody please!'

Blood slabbered from the cat's mouth her misshapen teeth chunking down on slivers of flesh.

When it was over, she licked the blood from her whiskers and dropped her tail down as she slunk into the gloom. The skies were clotted with purple clouds, and you could hear the chatter of old men praying over the wind.

Saira Viola is the author of Jukebox and Crack Apple &Pop. She is a multiple Pushcart Prize and Best of The Net nominee. Her fiction and poetry have appeared in Vautrin Magazine, International Times, Mü Magazine several other publications, and the latrine walls of The Little Red Door Paris.

HILARY SPIERS

HINKYPUNK

It was a thin, mean, cheese-paring moon. A moon that could barely rouse itself to shine. Feeble as French mustard. I deserved better. A full-blooded, sky-filling moon that dripped magic. A moon that glowed sharp as frost in the velvet heavens. (I was in a romantic mood that night.) A witness moon. Who's to say how differently things might have turned out had I got it?

It is not a night for romance – not under these clouds. It is a night for mischief. People will be abroad, awake, long after their normal bedtimes tomorrow but tonight most are slumbering uneasily, twitching bedclothes in the witching hour, quarrelling with themselves in the deep recesses of their troubled minds. A nation twisting and turning in the labyrinths of sleep, save for the night-workers, toiling through the dark, an unlucky few bothered by sudden irruptions of bright-eyed politicians, fizzing with Red Bull. In castle and tenement, moated grange and humble semi, the people fret and mutter, listening now to the heart, now to the head. Ripe pickings for a wayward spirit. The last few hours to pry and prod and prick.

Sir Milton Goldworthy, prime specimen of the squirearchy, smiles and snores smug as a self-satisfied bug in his vast bed, visions of his pert-buttocked PA warming his dreams, heedless of constituents who, lamb-like, trot to vote for him, year on unchanging year. Beside him, wakeful in the fuggy room, lies Mildred, wondering where the years and her figure have gone. She wishes the night away, fingers itching to make her mark defiantly, secretly, against another name. I trail a breath across her frowning forehead and she slaps her husband's ample rump. That's for his snoring. And his PA.

Across the country I surge and dart, a doubt dropped here, a certainty unseated there. In the wild, wet west, Caroline

Burtonstock, independent minded and unaffiliated, but angry to the marrow of her bones, stares out upon the distant moon-dribbled hills and worries for her children should the polls deceive and by some miracle she wins. She shivers as I run a finger down her doubting spine and feels the first stirrings of hope. She can always get a nanny.

'They're all a bunch of scoundrels,' says Bernard Copstick to no one in particular, as the landlord turfs out the last few stragglers from The Dozy Duck. Bernard's fellow sots across the land mutter their agreement and weave their befuddled way through the various ginnels and twitchells of their villages towards a night of rumpled, crumpled sheets and indecision. I whisper in ears and insinuate beguiling choices in dithering, wavering minds. Panic flares like heartburn in breasts that never felt the chill finger of equivocation before. My needling, puckish finger.

The night wears on, beneath its pallid sentinel, as I traverse complacent shires, swoop over ugly urban sprawls, glide along suburbs hedged with conflict and roam the windy northern wastes, laying my jittery, spiky grenades.

3 am. Sir Milton stirs, the first faint whiff of danger in the air. He pulls the eiderdown higher round his neck and kicks at something nameless coiled around his feet. A hundred miles away, his leader, hollow-eyed, is studying the entrails of the latest polls. 'There's a chill in here,' he grumbles, 'Has someone left a window open?' Acolytes run to shut out the damp night air that I let in, along with the spectre of something they would rather not consider.

In Downing Street, lights burn to scare away the shadows. They don't scare me. I chase exhausted aides along corridors that smell of Pledge with a subtle top note of fear. 'Go to bed,' they urge their master, but I stir up the dark forces of superstition and stubbornness and those two dread sisters fly to my side, eager for the fray. They wave me on my way, settling proprietorially in the hall.

'What the hell's happening?' yells an editor to journos reading runes and blogs and tweets, coffee cooling in mountainous paper cups on desks awash with figures and formulas and coming up with nothing tangible. Or nothing tangible that's fit to print. The rolling news jars and judders, speculates and supposes and then does what it always does. Invents. 'Whose side are we on again?' queries a grizzled hack who's seen too many contests to be either surprised or interested. 'The winning side,' barks his boss.

The moon begins its apologetic wane, as a couple used to disappointment lie side by side and wide awake in their comfortable Laura-Ashleyed bedroom, studying the ceiling.

'Scared?' she says. She squeezes his hand under the covers. From a room along the landing comes the cough of a fretful child.

'Apprehensive,' he says. 'Excited.' He corrects himself, 'Over-excited.' He checks his watch. 'Just after four. Twenty-four hours from now ...' They laugh softly, ruefully. 'Bless,' I think and almost weaken. Any other time, I would. But tonight's different, it's not a night for heartbreak and ecstasy. Or not that sort. I dust the couple with the shavings of disquiet: I doubt they'll notice, they're used to that.

Three hours to go. I redouble my efforts. Now here, now there, now east, now west, I dance in dreams and rattle nerves, sow unsettling seeds and scatter shards of ambiguity that catch the wind and chime discordantly. The nation's skin erupts and itches.

Muriel Chambers is not so easily spooked. Muriel and I are old acquaintances, we've jousted many times before and she is waiting for me. Upright in her chair, white hair gleaming in the fading moonlight, she is sitting out the night.

'I might have known it,' she says without turning her face from the window. 'I might have known it was you.' I settle at her feet and wait.

'Up to no good again, Will?' She gives a short bitter laugh. 'As if I needed to ask.'

'Do you blame me?' I say. 'With this shower?'

'You're a fine one to talk, bad lot that you are,' she counters.

'Ah,' I say. 'But I don't pretend to be otherwise.' We sit in silence contemplating the purity of my misdeeds.

'Well, what's happening out there?' she asks. So, I tell her. About the Milton Goldworthys,

the Caroline Burtonstocks, the Bernard Copsticks and the rest. I tell her about the anger and

the despair, the desperation, the lies, the subterfuges and the frail, faint shoots of hope. She

looks at me with all the wisdom of her ninety years and snorts her disbelief.

'Change?' she says. 'All I can say is, if it's coming, it's taken its time.'

Then I'm off again, out of her antimacassared and chintzy room in the ironically named Happy Havens Retirement Home, calling up my fellow mischief-makers for one last, glorious spree, unseating expectations and tickling secret fancies in the breasts of couples who long ago forgot how to talk to each other. This dawn, the wilting moon holds no sway over us; we sashay to a different tune. Fitful sleepers twitch their way through vivid, catastrophic dreams. Mist licks the river edge, hovers in the dells and valleys of this fair and troubled land. Streetlights flicker and go out and, as milkmen rattle their bottles in deserted avenues, the exhausted populace, more lost, more indecisive, more confused than ever, wakes.

In polling stations, lists and ballot papers are straightened, pencils aligned, and the first of many sour coffees sipped. Workers hover impatiently outside, anxious to do their civic duty and get back to their routines. None however can quell the little shiver of excitement and sense of self-importance as they enter the confessional. But I and my like are there too, crowding them, plucking at their consciences, stirring with wicked fingers their muddied thoughts. Pencils skitter over names, they hover, retreat, advance and suddenly score a cross. People stagger out, dumbfounded, discomfited. They wave away the eager officials brandishing clipboards and stumble on their way.

Sir Milton arrives in his fiefdom, oozing complacency, and flourishes his ballot for the waiting press. Lady Mildred, heart in overdrive, boldly makes her mark against another name, a woman, gay and black, and has to rearrange her face into a dutiful smile before she takes her place beside her spouse. Her serviceable handbag, alas, catches the PA a bruising blow upon her sculpted thighs.

Caroline Burtonstock and her children walk to school, open today not for education, but for democracy. It's important for them to see these things in action, she thinks. Lucy Burtonstock, five, tugs the sleeve of a woman in the queue. 'Have you come to vote for my Mummy?' she asks. The woman recognises Caroline from the local paper and thinks, 'Why not? She looks nice. And what a sweet little girl.'

Bernard Copstick forgets to take his glasses and votes for the wrong candidate. Hope flowers in the breasts of the couple used more to scorn than adulation as the numbers start to climb and shell-shocked candidates muster sickly smiles for the cameras.

And still I do not rest, creeping along byways, hugging the shadows, to nudge a floater, pinch a doubter. Grumbling, they reach for their voting cards and set off, chivvying their neighbours to follow suit. Queues spring up suddenly, blocking pavements, and startled volunteers harass returning officers about a shortage of forms. Postal voters turn up in person, adding to the turmoil. And all the while the pundits ponder, old stagers utter platitudes and markets tremble.

Muriel Chambers takes her time. She listens to The Archers at 7.03, tutting at the rural shenanigans and reaches for her coat. Still sprightly and armed with a stick used more for others' reassurance than her own, she sets off the few hundred yards to the local Community Centre. She doesn't falter as she passes me, whispering blandishments through the letterbox of a first-time voter who hasn't. Yet.

She looks up at the moon struggling to be seen through the ash. 'Early tonight, aren't you?' she says.
I laugh. Thousands hear the echo and remember with a jolt what they still need to do before 10pm.

'You're looking very pleased with yourself, you little devil,' she says.

'Devil!' I exclaim. 'That's nice! Don't you know who I am?'

Muriel fixes me with a weary look. ''Course I do. Jack-a-Lantern, ELLYLLDAN, WILL O' THE WISP –

TROUBLE, IN ANY LANGUAGE.'

'NOT TONIGHT,' I SAY. 'TONIGHT I'M ON THE SIDE OF THE ANGELS. THE PEOPLE'S FRIEND. THEIR

CHAMPION. WILL OF THE PEOPLE.'

AND AS THE MOON FINALLY BREAKS THROUGH THE GATHERING CLOUDS, I'M GONE. JOB DONE.
UNTIL THE NEXT TIME.

BREAD AND SALT

The sun. Brutal on their unprotected heads when they ventured onto the balcony. The humidity. Inescapable. Gluing their clothes – synthetics mainly; they hadn't time to pack anything but what was to hand – to their sweating bodies. The ageing, creaking ceiling fan a mockery, flies floating in its feeble draught.

The food too. Strange, hot – why, for Chrissakes, in this heat? – speckled with unidentifiable bits of leaf or God knows what. At first, she pushed it away, its pungent smell exacerbating a persistent nausea she could not shift. Until finally she recognised it as homesickness. Heart-sickness. Hunger drove her to try it, a tiny spoonful at a time, until her mouth became inured to the taste. She dreamt of burgers.

And the dust. In eyes, eyelashes, ears, crevices of her body she did not believe it could discover. Her skin, hair, tongue even, coated with it.

'I hate it here,' she whispered to Marnie's back one night, almost soundlessly, no more than an exhalation, willing her both to hear and not. Marnie, lost in sleep, moaned, eyelids fluttering. 'We should have stayed. Risked it.'

Home. Rain. Wet pavements. Gutters bubbling like rivers, rubbish whirling down to block the drains. A skim of petrol on puddles, iridescent under a cold winter sun. The smell of the city: dirty, sour. Beloved. The longing dragged at her belly like sex.

***

'I have your applications,' says Achmed, perched on their grubby sofa, brogued feet crossed demurely at the ankles. He has left their apartment door slightly ajar, as he always does. On his first visit, Marnie had padded across the concrete floor to close it, only for him to rise and re-open it without a word, carefully edging the bolt to kiss the metal plate but not click shut.

Eyes downcast, the girls wait. It had been one of the first things Achmed had explained to them in his faultless, barely accented English. 'Do not look a man in the eye. Until he speaks to you. Outside the home, I mean. But you can look at me!' He had smiled, willing them to relax their stolid expressions. When they didn't, his face had tightened. 'It is considered disrespectful.'

He scans a slim file, thin fingers running down a checklist. Finally, he says with something between disappointment and relief, 'Ah! Yes, as I thought. We are still awaiting information. The British authorities –'

'Christ! We've been here three months! Three months! We've told you everything – last time you came, you said, just be patient, it takes time –'

'It does,' he says gently, spreading his hands in regret. 'Without passports –'

Bev slams her fist onto the sofa. 'How many times?! They took them. They stole them, the people smugglers. They had guns: what were we supposed to do?'

'Shh ...' Marnie slips an arm around her shoulders. It lies heavy as a chain across her neck.

Achmed shrugs, not, she knows, uncaringly but because he is powerless. They are only two in hundreds that he deals with day on day, a tide of misery stowing away, walking, hobbling, swimming, as fast as they can away from a Europe in flames. He is always courteous but she senses the other responsibilities stacked up at the door awaiting his attention the second he finishes with them.

He checks his watch constantly, his discomfort palpable. She is suddenly embarrassed by her bare legs in the faded shorts, her skimpy tee-shirt. Marnie now drifts around the cramped apartment in a voluminous kaftan – that's what they'd call it back home; they'll have another word for it over here, another strange, unpronounceable word – that came in a bag of castoffs. Achmed had brought it with him on his first visit, explaining gently, almost apologetically, that most refugees were issued with such a bag. It is our tradition, he had said. To welcome the stranger, take them to our hearts. They knew they should be grateful but were not.

When Achmed leaves, Marnie returns to the bedroom where she lies day after day, staring at the ceiling. Bev yanks the tatty plastic carrier, its H&M logo faded almost to oblivion, out from under sofa and scrabbles through it. The clothes give off a chemical smell as though they have all been washed together with no thought for colour or fabric. At the bottom of the bag, packed tight in the corner, she finds a balled garment, black. It is barely larger than her hand. As she shakes it out, it expands, billows in the slight breeze from the ceiling fan, its hem fluttering to the floor like a stream of dark water. She measures the garment against her tall frame, is surprised to find it reaches her feet. As she pulls it over her head, it floats down her body, the slithering silk delicate as a lover's touch. Shucking off her shorts, she strides into the tiny bathroom to the only mirror in the place, the air cool on her sticky thighs. Cockroaches scuttle into the corners as she throws the light switch. On tiptoe, she peers at the length of the garment in the mirror, turning this way and that, front, back, sides. A flaw catches her eye. Just under the left armpit, a flash of flesh. She pulls the fabric across her breast, sees the small tear, four or five millimetres at most. Just as she goes to remove the garment, she hears the bedroom door open. The dress is off in a moment. Marnie stumbles into the corridor en route to the toilet. She blinks under the electric light, the pallor of her skin accentuated in the unnatural brightness. She doesn't even look at Bev, the dress scrunched up behind her, just squats over the lavatory and pisses with a grunt. They've got used to the lack of toilet paper. Marnie washes her hands under the cold tap, gives them a cursory dry on the threadbare towel and, using the rough wall for support, staggers back to the bedroom, leaving behind a faint smell of sweat and urine.

Back in the lounge, Bev picks over the other garments. Three blouses, a length of vivid red satin, a handful of headscarves, four bras in different sizes. She smoothes out the scarves: paisley, spotted, plain, one sporting camels, soft and filmy under her fingers. A thought. For the first time in months, a sense of excitement. Silently, she pads back towards the bathroom.

***

It isn't easy. The scissors in her little sewing kit are useless. After a few minutes, she abandons caution and simply tears the fabric, surprised to see how straight it rips. What was that expression? Going with the grain? Ribbons of colour gather in a pile beside her.

She doesn't know why she doesn't tell Marnie about her project. Cannot explain why she bundles the garment under the sofa cushion when she hears her coming and sits on it, heart beating wildly. It's exhilarating having a secret, that's all she knows. It fills a small corner in her aching heart.

There is no news from home. Without their phones, the women are wholly dependent on Achmed. Once, he brings them an old Daily Mail, but it's from before they fled, its news no news at all, just faux reassurances from politicians mouthing platitudes as they lose their grip on a country in chaos. Bev finds the images of her old life, their friends, their flat, starting to fade. It panics her. She tries to picture their bookshelves: she and Marnie were – are – both voracious readers, but the titles elude her, along with the authors. 'What's the name of that book about the neurosurgeon? There's a march? A kidnapping?' Marnie shakes her head. She asks Achmed on his next visit. 'Saturday,' he says immediately, 'Ian McEwen.' They beg him for books. 'I'll try,' he says. But he has more important things to worry about. They don't ask a second time. Instead, they try to recall their favourite novels but find themselves muddling one plot with another, arguing about characters, motives, dénouements. They haven't had a proper conversation in weeks. Each day merges with the next in a fog of inactivity and waiting.

Outside, building work goes on relentlessly, night and day, bulldozers clearing the rubble of a thousand air strikes, women and boys picking over the ruins of homes for anything that can be salvaged and re-used. The only respite from the noise is the call to prayers. Bev learns to love the pure unaccompanied voice silencing the clamour, the flow of the notes rising and falling through the still air. She asks Achmed what the muezzin is singing. As he tells her about the adhan, his face is transformed. She envies him that certainty, that belief. On yet another fruitless visit, he brings her a copy of the Quran in English. When she finds Marnie reading it one morning, she feels hot with anger, betrayed. 'That's mine,' she says and Marnie hands it to her without a word, retreats silently to the bedroom. Without the solace of books each day is bleached of meaning. Without books, there is no escape.

Marnie, once so close, not just a sister but her best friend, is drifting away from her like a boat carried out on the tide. Bev has taken to the roof at night, pleading the heat, the stickiness of their shared bed. Under the stars, she's more aware than ever of the beat of the city's heart, the throng of humanity all around her, breathing the same air, dreaming the same dreams. It lulls her to a restless sleep, punctuated by the grind of machinery far below, the darkness pierced by the construction arc lights. At dawn, the muezzin wakes her and the city starts its daily cycle, the cries of children mingling with the clash of cooking pots, the shouts of the street vendors.

She and Marnie pass like strangers in the corridor. Each closes the bathroom door now when they wash or use the toilet. Bev starts to use the rooftop in the daytime now, fashioning a crude shelter from a blanket tied between two pipes. Cross-legged on a sofa cushion, her back against the wall, she reads the Quran over and over, treasuring each word. Otherwise, she stitches the dress. Scraps of torn silk become flowers, butterflies, the edges meticulously oversewn; she appliqués them in a cluster at the hem, drawing the thread through the fabric in a slow, steady rhythm, repairs the small tear with tiny stitches until it is barely visible.

Then one day, around lunchtime, she descends in search of food and, entering the apartment, knows immediately that she is alone, her sister's absence an accusation. She searches every room, light-headed, heart hammering. The bed is empty, Marnie's few clothes gone, the missing toothbrush in the mug a reproach. Exactly half their pitiful savings remain in the coffee jar. She runs onto the balcony.

Below the window, the streets seethe with people; there's no sign of a slight figure in a shabby kaftan slipping through the crowds. The scale of Marnie's folly almost undoes her. She stumbles downstairs. In a mixture of sign language and the few words of Arabic she has acquired, Bev persuades the old gatekeeper to let his grandson take a message to Achmed at the Ministry; her hand is unsteady as she scrawls the note, the taste of guilt bitter in her mouth.

'Where did she go?' demands Achmed, less than an hour later, flustered, sweaty, caught on the hop. His anxiety makes him sound shrill, emasculates him. Bev, crouched on the sofa, shakes her head, looking up at him as he stands over her.

'There is a note? Yes?' His fluency seems to have deserted him. No, she says tonelessly, no note. Only her clothes and a little money gone.

'She cannot get far.' He says this somewhere between a statement and a plea for reassurance. She has none to give him. 'They will find her.' He doesn't elucidate who 'they' are. He quizzes her rapidly, eyes never leaving her face: had they quarrelled, had she shown any signs of wanting to leave, were there any unreported visitors ...? She senses an untethering of his usual reserve, as though the veneer of cosmopolitan acceptance of their invasion of his world, their constant badgering, their neediness, has been masking a distaste he has been too polite to express. Perhaps he will be blamed for Marnie's disappearance: one of his sheep straying. He says savagely, 'You will come with me. Now.'

'Out?' says Marnie, bewildered. They have been immured in this tiny space ever since they arrived, obedient to his insistence that they do not leave. Not until their position is regularised, their status determined.

'Quick,' barks Achmed, mouth tight with tension. He looks with undisguised contempt at her thin cotton skirt, the strappy top. He puts out a hand to pull her to her feet. She pushes herself upright. 'Wait.'

It lies spilt on the rumpled bed where she had thrown it in her panic. She strips to her underwear and slips the dress over her head. The decoration at the hem gives the fabric an added weight; it swirls around her legs then settles. She buttons it to the neck, is about to return to the lounge, throwing back her unloosed hair. She stops. On a chair lies one of the silk scarves that survived her tearing spree. It is black. She ties it under her chin, then knots the ends at the back of her neck.

'Oh!' Achmed stares at her in consternation.

She lowers her eyes. He crosses the room, pulls the fabric a little further down her forehead. She can smell garlic and onions on his breath.

He smiles boyishly, the old Achmed for a second. 'Good. This is good. Come.' He ushers her out into the stairwell, pulling the apartment door shut behind him. They have no keys. They have never had keys.

The light is blinding in the street doorway, the air thick with smells – dung, bread, blood, smoking fat. The noise astounds her. She had thought the apartment noisy but here at street level, the cacophony hits her like a physical blow. Achmed, already forging a path through the crowds, turns back to where she hesitates on the threshold, suddenly afraid. 'Come!'

Bev shrinks back into the shadows, mouth dry, heart pulsing. The press of the people ... she hasn't been out in months, not since that journey in the open truck from the reception centre. Not since she and Marnie, terrified, had held hands like children, despite the sour expression of the rifle-toting guard at the tailgate, needing that touch of comfort amidst this strange and disorienting turmoil, the officials' brisk coldness contrasting with the smiling people they passed, waving, gesturing welcome. At a crossroads, a boy had run up to the truck, brandishing a large object and thrust it at her. Her first thought, as it fell into her lap, and the guard leapt to his feet, shouting and levelling his gun at the boy, was a bomb. So used had they become back home to the ambushes, the booby-traps, the bloody dangers lurking on every street corner, that they braced themselves for the blast, even as she swept the bundle to the floor. Its covering fell away, exposing the contents.

A loaf. Bread. The stuff, the staff, of life.

By the time she had raised her dazed face to the street, the guard, muttering, subsiding in his seat, the boy was lost in the throng. 'Why don't they hate us?' she had whispered to Marnie as they tore into the yielding dough.

Later, much later, she had asked Achmed the same question. 'You are guests in our country,' he had said, slightly puzzled. 'It is our duty to welcome the stranger.'

Now he is holding out a hand, nodding understandingly. His eyes are kind. Bev takes a deep breath, pushes away from the wall, and slips her hand into his. One step, two, like learning to walk again. Achmed leads her through the mass of bodies, and no-one stares, no-one pays her any attention. She is no more than a speck in this vast crowd, invisible.

Her feet are sore, soles on fire from the friction of tender skin, unused to walking, against the leather. The top straps bite into her flesh. Once, she loses a sandal, lets go of Achmed's hand to ferret blindly for it in the dust, only to feel her foot squelch on something soft and yielding. Achmed stops, turns back, eyebrows knitted in anger.

'What?'

'My shoe.' She doesn't want to examine her foot, insinuates it gingerly back under the strap and grits her teeth against the pain and disgust as slimy sole slips on leather. Achmed peers ahead, his western-clad form alien in this sea of robes. Figures, male and females, skirt him warily and hurry on their way, as he starts off again. In a shadowy doorway, an old man chewing khat, eyes jumping, hawks a gob of mucus as Achmed passes; it lands at her feet. She pulls her scarf a little further forward and scurries on in Achmed's wake, sandals stirring the gritty dust. 'Please,' she calls, but her voice is lost in clamour. She picks up speed, earns a curse from a trader repairing his display of mangoes as she catches his arm. One fat fruit spills from his fingers and rolls in her path; she leaps over it, ignoring a volley of shouts behind her, running now in a heart-clutching lurch to catch up with her protector. When she does, she snatches at his shirtsleeve, almost throws herself into his arms, tears welling.

'You've seen her?' His face lights up. Eyes dart back the way they have come.

'No. Please. I can't ...' She doubles over, clutching her side. When she looks up, he is expressionless, but for a flash of what she reads as contempt. Then he takes her arm, more gently than she expects. 'Come.' At a nearby stall, he buys two tiny bitter coffees, hands her one. She steadies herself, resisting the impulse to use him as a crutch, waits for him to speak first. Achmed knocks his coffee back in one gulp.

'I didn't ask,' he says. 'Have you a picture?'

'Oh!' She hands him her cup, scrambles in her cloth bag, Achmed moving automatically in front of her to shield her from view. In her purse, a rather dog-eared snap taken in a tube station photo booth three, four, years ago, after a night out. The pair of them, both slightly dishevelled, flushed with alcohol, hugging and grinning into the camera. The only picture of Marnie she now owns, all the others lost when her phone was taken from her. She remembers the weight and yield of her sister's buttocks in her lap, the softness of her body as she wrapped her arms around her. The memory skewers her.

Achmed examines the photo, frowns. Before she can stop him, in one swift movement he tears around Marnie's face, excises Bev from the picture, tosses the curling fragment aside, her tattered image discarded like so much garbage. As she lunges for it, a gust of wind catches it and it dances out of her reach, lost in the crowd. She cries out, not words, but the meaning unmistakeable, loss tempered with anger, the last thread to the time before this nightmare shorn.

'What?' says Achmed with a belligerence that betrays his guilt, skin reddening.

'It was ... it was ...' She can't get the words out, is beyond explanation, feels the last vestiges of hope drain away. They'll never find Marnie now, not in this press of humanity, these impenetrable allies and doorways. On foot, she's an hour, perhaps two, ahead of them. In a vehicle (and here bile rises to her throat), who knows? It's hopeless.

She rallies. 'No-one would recognise her from that. She's thinner ... her hair is ...' She stops. Surely Marnie would have thought to cover her head? This wasn't a spur-of-the-moment decision; she had been edging away – they both had – for weeks. The pitiful balance in the jar, the toothbrush gone from the bathroom. Not a moment of madness but a conscious, planned decision. How despairing must she have been, how certain that she could no longer count on that tie of blood, that shared history? If Marnie has disappeared, she means it, doesn't want to be found. Either that, or life had become so intolerable, she doesn't care what happens, just wants something to happen. Guilt twists her guts.

'So?' says Achmed, challenging her to take responsibility. But how can she? She doesn't know this city, these people, can't imagine how a stranger could negotiate her way safely to ... to where?

Suddenly, someone is at Achmed's elbow, tugging. He slides a look at Bev: she recognises him immediately. The grandson from downstairs. The boy looks scared. Achmed bends so the boy can whisper in his ear. He jerks upright as the boy sprints away back the way he had come, swallowed instantly by the crowd.

Achmed seizes her elbow, spilling the last drops of her coffee. He shoves her cup at the vendor, then steers her back into the throng. His face is set, determined.

'What did he say? Does he know where she is? Where are we going?'

Achmed does not reply, just surges through the bodies, his free hand here to move someone aside, a shoulder there angled to slip through a gap, pulling her after him. Faces, eyes, flash past. They stumble along for several minutes in the same awkward posture, both of them slightly off balance.

The street narrows. They are in the old town now, she realises. No obvious sign of any damage here. Shabby buildings, paint peeling, crowd the space at drunken angles, elaborate balconies festooned with drying laundry flapping overhead. Abruptly, he stops, looks up at the lintel of a gateway, nods. People surge around them, annoyed by the unexpected blockage. There are grunts of exasperation, muttered asides. Still gripping her elbow, Achmed marches her across to a doorway deep in shadow, barred by an ornate iron gate. He pushes a button; distantly, a bell tinkles.

She squints through the bars trying to see beyond the blackness of the passageway, at length making out what looks like a small courtyard. Just as her eyes adjust, the sight is blotted out by the silhouette of an approaching figure. A hand emerges from a floor-length robe and inserts a large key into the lock. The door swings open inwards.

Bev waits for Achmed to precede her. He does not move. She feels a hand upon her wrist, is eased gently into the passageway, the gate clanging shut behind her, then the unmistakeable sound of a key being turned. Looking back, she sees Achmed the other side of the bars, his face unreadable, a hand raised in farewell. A man slips in front of him and when she blinks, Achmed is gone.

The woman, enveloped in black, only her eyes visible, still has hold of her wrist, her hand warm on Bev's dusty skin; it slips down until their fingers are interlaced and Bev can feel the gritty friction of their palms. She is lead on towards the sunlight. They step into the courtyard.

To one side, three spiral-stemmed olive trees. To the other, an ancient stone fountain. A bird perches on the rim, inspecting the new arrivals. The sunlight is dazzling. It takes Bev a few seconds to realise that all she can hear is the soft splashing of water; no cries of hawkers, no screech of traffic, no scuffle of feet. It is like the silence of snow, muffling the present, an otherworldliness. The bird takes off from the fountain, the sound of its wings assaulting the still air.

The woman releases Bev's hand, gestures across the courtyard towards another archway. Bev limps across to find herself in a smaller, more ornate enclosure, tessellated floor, gilded pillars of veined marble, the space edged with stone benches on which plump embroidered cushions rest. In the centre, a small pool, tiled in mosaics of blue and green, depicting dolphins and mythical sea creatures. The air is scented with rose petals, a handful of which floats on the water. At the woman's silent invitation, she sinks on to a cushion, too exhausted to frame her thoughts into anything except the need for rest. Her head is filled with a persistent beat: Marnie, Marnie, Marnie ... But for the moment, she cannot take another step. Muscles shudder with fatigue. Her eyes close.

Hands untie her scarf, then moving down her arms, touch her knees and reach her feet. Feather-light, they prise the sandals from her swollen, bloodied feet, then gently, gently, lift them into a bowl of warm water. She feels boneless, fragile. If she keeps her eyes closed, the world cannot get in. A comb is drawn with infinite tenderness through her tangled hair; she tips her head back, surrenders. Vaguely, she is aware of words – a prayer? – being breathed into her ear and, like a picture slowly coming into definition, she sees herself in another place, another time, head bowed in submission as the priest lays the Host on her tongue. The smell of the incense, the echo of footsteps on the old stone flags, the familiar chill of the ancient walls. All that she is, was, in that long-ago moment, a life preserved in amber. Then, everything had seemed eternal, immutable. Who would not believe it all – the building, the traditions, the sanctuary it offered – would last forever? Such complacency, such folly. Would it even be there any longer, that old church? So many had been bombed, desecrated, vandalised, leaving nothing but rubble and dust. And now, here, beneath her feet in their cocoon of soothing water, tiny fragments of a different dust, chafing her tender skin. Heat, even in the shade, still heavy on her limbs. Unfamiliar scents. The strangeness of it all. Foreign, alien, other. A tear trembles in one eye, spills. She tastes the salt as she licks it away.

Her companion speaks. Bev opens her eyes, looks into those of the other woman. Brown, deep, weathered by age. Eyes that have known both sorrow and laughter.

'Thank you,' says Bev. The woman shakes her head: it was nothing. She holds out her hand and Bev takes it, rising unsteadily. Grit swirls in the water as she lifts her feet clear of the rim and steps onto a towel laid beside the bowl. The woman lifts her arms and is drawing the silk gown over her head, unclipping her bra. Unbidden, Bev shucks off her pants and at a nod from her companion, gingerly makes her way down the curved stone steps into the pool. There is no shame, no embarrassment. Bev tips her head back, lets the warm, scented water lap around her hair as it haloes around her. The sky above is cloudless, blue as the Virgin's robe. She hears the slap of the woman's sandals receding until there is only the gentle slop of the water on the edges of the pool.
She surrenders to the water's embrace. Slowly, the tumbling images behind her eyelids – parents, friends, the texture of a particular dress, the feel of a door-key in her palm, a bus's fumes, the splash of rain on her head – still. Stepping at length from the pool, she makes her way back to the bench across the hot tiles. A folded white towel lies beside a brass tray bearing a glass of water, a dish of salt and a piece of bread. It smells irresistible. She dips the bread into the salt and takes a bite. It tastes of companionship, a life just out of reach. She wraps herself in the towel, droplets on her shoulders already drying in the heat. Silence blankets the courtyard and the now motionless pool. All she can hear is the sound of her own breathing as she consumes the food like a sacrament. She aches under the weight of her loneliness.

Beneath the stone bench, she spots a pair of beaded slippers and slides her feet into them. Only then does she see her dress spread out on the adjacent bench in the full sun like a sacrifice, fresh white underwear beside it. She slips them on, inhaling the sweet laundered smell.

Her slippers glide soundlessly over the tiny tiles as she makes her way towards the cloister. In the doorway, she looks left and right; her nostrils catch a scent, instantly familiar but elusive. She sniffs again. Now she has it. Books. The smell of paper and print. The smell of freedom.

The room is vast. Fluted pillars soar to a ceiling decorated in vivid colours and gold leaf. Ancient images of women nursing babies, fighting, running, staring boldly at the viewer, cover every wall between bookshelves crammed with books of all descriptions. Tattered paperbacks sit alongside huge, leather-bound tomes, gold-tooled classics shoulder-to-shoulder with runs of learned journals. And in neat rows the whole length of the space, dozens of desks occupied by women, old, young, girls even, uncovered heads bowed intently over their reading material, some busily scribbling in notebooks, some leaning dreamily on one hand, lost in their secret worlds. Several women look up at the figure hovering on the threshold and smile or nod, before returning to their occupation. One bent head, though, snags her eye: red hair a flame in that sea of black. She blinks. Looks again. Her heart bucks in her chest. Marnie raises her head; their eyes lock. Carefully marking her place, Marnie rises, welcome, forgiveness, reconciliation in the deep pools of her eyes. She walks the length of her row and takes her sister's hand.

DAVID BRAMWELL

NELLIE BLY

The journalist who flew into the cuckoo's nest

It's the winter of 1887, and in New York's municipal lunatic asylum on Blackwell Island a new inmate is being subjected to the humiliation and discomfort of an ice-cold bath.

'I began to protest. My teeth chattered and my limbs were gooseflesh and bruised with cold. Suddenly I got ice cold water in my ears, nose and mouth. They dragged me out gasping, shivering and quaking, from the tub.'

–Ten Days in a Mad-house (1887)

The young woman had been at the asylum only for a few days and found it to be one of the most unpleasant experiences of her life. Since the first night, she had been unable to sleep because of the hard bed and screams of other patients. She was appalled by the rancid food and frightened by the sadistic nature of many of the nurses and doctors. She witnessed patients bound together with rope and found some who appeared to be there for no other reason than their poverty or inability to speak English. Some of the women, she discovered to her horror, had been committed by cruel husbands wanting to be rid of them.

Like Randle McMurphy in One Flew over the Cuckoo's Nest, the woman was no ordinary inmate. She had faked her own insanity in order to get access to the asylum. Not for an easy ride, as McMurphy had foolishly hoped, but to investigate and expose the abuse of patients. For the fearless journalist Nellie Bly, this was the big scoop.

Bly was born Elizabeth Jane Cochran in 1864, in a wealthy Pennsylvanian family, and enjoyed writing from an early age. After moving to Pittsburgh in 1880, she read an article in her local paper *The Pittsburgh Dispatch* by a popular columnist, Erasmus Wilson. Wilson, a tiresome misogynist wrote that 'the working woman is a monstrosity' and went on to bloviate that women should not get 'fancy ideas about educating themselves'.

Cochran, choking back her morning cereal, wrote a brilliantly caustic response to the paper, signing herself 'Little Orphan Girl'. Impressed, the editor tracked her down and offered her a job. She took the pen-name 'Nellie Bly' (after a popular song of the day) and began to write her own column, exposing the poor working conditions for women in a local factory, and calling for reform of the country's divorce laws. Naturally, she ruffled a few feathers and before long found herself being relegated to cover the more 'feminine' topics of fashion and gardening.

Bly quit, relocated to New York and, after four tireless months of challenging the patriarchal institution of journalism, landed a job at the New York World. It came with a caveat. To prove her worth, the editor asked Bly for a report on Blackwell's lunatic asylum, housed on an island off Manhattan. No one anticipated her level of commitment to the article. Taking the name of a Cuban immigrant, Nellie Brown, she rented a room in a brownstone tenement and began to act insane. She claimed to hear voices, had conversations with ghosts and within a few days successfully acted her way into Blackwell's, fooling an array of doctors, specialists and a court judge. 'It is a human rat trap. Easy to get in, once in, it's impossible to get out,' she would later write in her book, Ten Days in a Mad-house (1887).

After ten days Bly was released from Blackwell's when an agent from New York World came to collect her and prove (with some effort) that she was sane. Bly's exclusive exposé not only made her name, but instigated a full report on Blackwell's, leading to a million-dollar investment from the state and the promise that only the seriously mentally ill would be sent there in the future.

From here on in, Bly continued to delve into what her (jealous) fellow hacks named 'stunt' journalism. One week she was in a diving bell at the bottom of the ocean; the next she was undercover, exploring police corruption and the plight of unwanted babies. Then, in 1890, she persuaded the New York World to fund her on a round-the-world trip in an attempt to beat Phileas Fogg's fictional 80-day journey. As a single woman travelling alone, the journey would be an achievement in itself. Women were expected to take everything but the kitchen sink and half a dozen servants when travelling abroad; Bly simply packed two small bags and off she went.

During her 25,000-mile (4,000km) adventure she travelled by coach, train, rickshaw, horse, Chinese sampan and donkey. In France, she met author Jules Verne who saluted her heroic odyssey and gave her his favourite Breton shirt. She returned to America an even bigger hero. When Bly's name accompanied a newspaper headline, sales doubled.

Bly married Robert Seaman in 1894. She was 31; he was a 73-year-old millionaire running a company that made steel cans and barrels clad in iron. The company bore the imaginative name of Ironclad. Unsurprisingly, Seaman conked out a few years later and Bly took over the business. She worked hard to give the workers better rights and improve their working conditions, even building them a library for self-education. After an unfortunate case of fraud and embezzlement, however, Bly lost her husband's fortune. She left for Europe, intending to take a vacation but, still a journalist at heart, stayed there for five years as a First World War correspondent.

Of course, Bly wasn't going to do her reporting from behind a desk; she followed the action to the front line, risking life and limb for her features. She returned to New York in 1919 and continued to write and give lecture tours around America, until her death, aged 57.

Nellie Bly paved the way for investigative journalism as we know it today, never afraid to risk her life and reputation to help change the world for the better. If she'd been alive today, Bly would doubtless have fronted ground-breaking gritty TV documentaries, making Louis Theroux and Michael Moore's work look like a wet weekend in comparison.

SAVITRI PEMA:

ZOOM CALLS FOR THE DEAD AND DYING

My nephew's tears stain his mask as he takes us all for a virtual tour of his mother's body, the camera shaking uncontrollably as it hovers over her face. Someone had placed a stem of the pinky white mango blossom at her feet. She loved the flowers so much she had even insisted on weaving some into her wedding garland when she got married. I had tried telling her that no-one did that, because of their sickly-sweet scent, but she had laughed and said she was going to do it anyway, because it was her special day. I recall also how much she had irritated me about a few sequins that had come loose on her wedding sari. Now the bright red clashes with the neon orange of the marigold garland draped around her neck, making me want to rip it off, to wake her out of her slumbering state: to smell her favourite flowers.

Sobbing and keening sounds emanate from the virtual mourners across the globe in Zoom windows connected like the cells within a beehive. The Indian diaspora has seeded across the globe, growing in numbers and stature over time from toiling at menial low paid jobs, to educating many of the successive generations as doctors; lawyers; businessmen and women: still connected to their roots, especially at times like this.

Guilt bubbles up inside me as I force myself to look at her serene face. Why her, and not me, I ask myself. What have I done to deserve to be saved from the same fate? But deep down I know. I have migrated to a country with care systems with sufficient resources to save me. Despite my repeated offers for her and her family to join us, she had refused, adamant that she did not want to live in the land of her country's oppressors. She was stubborn like that.

My sense of time and place unravels, the tableaux out of focus on the screen, to relive another funeral. My aunt had been laid out like her daughter on a wooden board. The priest had been chanting verses from our holy book the Gita, a cloud of pungent smoke from sandalwood incense sticks swirling over his head. The house had been full of relatives and at least one person from each household in our village had been there. Attending a funeral was considered a great poon, a blessing to take into your next life, redressing some of your paaps, your sins in the great karmic cycle of rebirth.

When it was time to hoist the corpse onto the shoulders of four male relatives to take to the cremation ghat, my cousin had flung herself onto her mother's body, insisting that she wanted to accompany her on the last journey. It was not allowed she was told, as they tried to prise her off, for women to witness the ritual burning of the temporary home of the soul. They said that although it was not forbidden according to any of the scriptures, it was against our parampara, our tradition. A tradition created by priests, to exclude women from another sphere of life.

Moved by her distress and emboldened by my feminist education in the West I had been vociferous in my support of her wishes. I had joined her, the heady smell of marigolds in my nostrils forever a memory of that day. No doubt fearful of the auspicious hour passing for the cremation, the priest had reluctantly conceded. We had won, creating a different tradition that day, not just for us, but for those women in our village who wanted to decide for themselves.

Now I touch my cousin's face on the screen and berate her inert form 'You cheated' I tell her. 'I'm the eldest. It should have been me first. Like it's always been.' Being a mere two months older than her, we had nevertheless vied throughout our lives, regaling each other with our little triumphs. I had beat her in graduating and getting a well-paid job, she in marrying and having children first. Now she had won the race that I had not even wanted to compete in. Regret washes over me, at how our last proper conversation had gone from a heated debate, to an argument about India's space programme.

'Just think about the possibility of valuable resources on the Moon and Mars, like platinum and gold. And helium, that could power a city like Mumbai for decades' she had sounded so excited, irritating me with her enthusiasm.

'So you're proud of being part of a system that's spending millions of rupees on space programmes, rather than housing and feeding the millions of poor people who live in slums, are you? For allowing children to scavenge for food in rubbish dumps, instead of being educated and having a childhood?' I had taunted her.

'Yes,' she had shot back 'I am proud. Proud that India has never invaded another country to steal resources and cheap labour for its own development. Our land has been depleted by successive regimes and has to provide the best it can for its citizens. But we can't fall behind in this race. We can't stand still whilst we try and solve our problems, and not have a stake in having the resources for future generations.'

I had been angry with her for challenging my Liberal western views, almost slamming the phone down.

One of so many in this tsunami of loss, today there is no priest present to intone the scriptures over my cousin's body. Another tradition that will not be observed. Instead, the technologically savvy younger generation are playing a recording of the funeral rites through a loudspeaker that can be heard by the handful of mourners seated outside in the courtyard.

The women are in their mourning white saris, and the men in snowy cotton kurtis over loose trousers. Heads bowed in deference they listen silently to verses in our ancient language Sanskrit, incomprehensible to most who have not studied it. The words are however comforting in their familiarity, dormant in our individual cells around the globe, connecting us to our collective identity. We repeat chants written more than six thousand years ago by sages and holy men, who themselves purported to have transcended human attachment; grief and sorrow. The verses promise the unshackling of rebirth for earthly mortals according to their karma. The scales of good and evil could tip one way or another: to be reborn as an animal; an insect to be trodden on, or in human form in perpetuity, to toil again and again.

Fatalism in the face of unequal odds is a comfort blanket for those afflicted, a necessary buffer for those less fortunate. My hope is that this pandemic serves as a wakeup call, for countries to work together at a global level, to tackle these issues. For we are all connected by our humanity, globally and individually. My cousin takes with her today a part of me, the bits that only she knew, of memories of dancing in the mango grove: carefree, heady with the scent of pungent white blush blossom. Full of the joy of life.

YALE GOULD

THE INCIDENT AT THE LAKE

In 1973, Doris "Dot" Bichler won both the Anathea Siddons Memorial High School's Annual Science Fair and the district wide *Mr. Prestidigitato*r Competition, hands down. No one even came close, which was not unusual because, it seemed to Doris, few ever had. She wowed the judges with a remarkable tri-fold exhibition debunking Uri Geller's spoon-bending stunt (and of The Paranormal, and clairvoyance in general) as unreplicable pseudo-science. And in doing so, she eliminated one more suspicion—apart from her size and wild red hair—for her peers to think her too strange, too weirdly intrusive for friendship.

For the time being, her prize and local celebrity were enough. She'd secured appearances on the Saturday morning Mister Prestidigitator Science TV Show, her heart beat faster to hear her mother talk-her-up for a change (*so proud of you, Dottie*) and she had gained a new friend in the ever popular Elaine Simonetti.

The production crew liked her—she was smart and articulate—so they kept her on as a regular. They smeared her acne with pancake makeup, and cinched her waist and breasts with straps; they provided her with chemises that tented her bulk and faded her fat into the black-and- white's of the TV screen. She was a clone of the high school kid next door—fresh faced and pony-tailed and eager, her startling nest of red hair tamed into a pomaded clutch; she bopped through the screen door of Mr. Prestidigitator's suburban kitchen, placed her school books on a corner of his counter, and asked him how he was today. He was today (as every day) middle-aged, white-shirted, absolutely pleasant, and wifeless. He was always glad to see her. And, as scripted, she approached—wide-eyed and girly—wondering what this or that arrangement of his kitchen equipment and bottles of ordinary household liquids had to do with *why it rains or buoyancy or the movement of fluids through the green stems of spectacular flowers or what we call photosynthesis*. The bigger words were emphatically repeated—with expressions of absolute wonder—and flew up, letter after letter, in a chiming calliope glissando, as the two of them—Doris Bichler and Mr. Prestidigitator—gazed awestruck while the words assembled by syllable and zoomed into focus above them.

She was never his comic relief, his ugly sidekick—but played the adolescent who'd cue him, ask him those scripted questions, and arrive at her own amazing conclusions. He knew so much, and she so little.

And so it went on, week after week, every Saturday morning for at least a year of mixing baking soda and vinegar or the like—when *don't try this at home became try this, it won't kill you, even with adult supervision*—bending over the stainless bowls, both of them symbiotic, mock-startled by the foam, and by the symbol CO2 that fluttered up to the top of your living room's TV screen, and the molecules of gas that smothered the candle flame.

He was like her father if he, the real one, had ever been near—his large, high forehead, light baritone, and rimless lenses. How kind he was; how odd his acted presence worked-out in performance, and in her imagination.

He vouched for her, and left it to her to lock-up the last door. They would let her dawdle on set, in the cutaway kitchen—situated on a counter stool, her schoolbooks spread out, her make-up cold-creamed away, and her sorry skin flawless in the smooth blur of the polished Formica. It was quieter here than at home, what with the cat rubbing at her calves, her mother noticing, and going full out about her weight. Wasn't Doris fucking *here at last*? Hadn't she won?

She closed the several books she'd opened, slid off the breakfast stool, and box-stepped onto the checkerboard of the Kentile floor. She could *step on a crack and break your mother's back* and forgive herself that sing-song because home was hardly home, *really*—she was in no hurry and had nowhere else to go.

But *here.*

You might make yourself a piece of Wonder toast, stir the Nescafe into a porcelain mug, do-up a roast in the wall oven, and present it *ta-dah* with the enormous Kiss-the-Cook mitts they'd hung just so on the wall hook—why not? They were real enough, those gloves—bright red and large as leprosy, but the oven door was false, and would not budge no matter how hard she tugged: three times—three to realize (she slapped her head) the fool she was, it was not real, and would just pull off, and how would she ever explain the damage?

She slipped off the mitts, and for a fantastic moment, was relieved her fingers—fat thumb and the pudgy four—still worked separately; she hung the gloves back on the hook near the oven door, placed perfectly just for the *show*—as the entire kitchen was all show and built to fit in the neat frame of an idiot box. Just as *she* was—undeniably 'a good fit,' six inches tall and proportional, depending on the vertical hold—and how much weight could that image contain, after all?

She wandered the set, familiar by now, but always slightly odd in its artifice and false fronts. She sat on a chrome and vinyl dinette chair, and stared out a fake window, its cyclorama enhanced by the relentlessly sunny day of Mr. Prestidigitator's painted neighborhood. She was entranced. She had only been intent on learning her lines and asking the right questions for his easy answers, nodding *yes-yes* and coming to her conclusions in simplistic, idiotic dialogues of cause and effect.

Now, an ordinary window, *an extraordinary window*, was the medium of her imagination—not in the arbitrary images that materialized from the voices in her head, but with a clear *second sight* of perceptible places, and people—if they ever dared to show.

She'd never seen the streets of her city from this height, and surely there were few terraced views from any vantage point—even the highest window—in her own neighborhood. But the painted view was of a cozy village, where slate rooftops overlapped the clapboard walls of adjacent buildings, and the bright green pommels of trees and shrubs puffed up perfectly on the sides of store-lined walkways and ballooned in the parks and commons and in the backyards of orderly houses. It was an earthbound aerial view of a thrumming, but strangely people-less place where anyone who appeared on this scene—but for the lack of company—might feel instantly at home.

Could she? Could she even have walked those streets to let herself into Mr. Prestidigitator's kitchen, pony-tailed and shrill and eager, her curiosity killing her to please know the reasons for everything, *anything*? *Who* was she? *Why* was she at all?

She might be the first to appear in this happily arid place and catch the disease of her TV character—her gawking innocence and idiot "golly" grin—from breathing the atmosphere of a paint-by-numbers neighborhood like this. She half-swiveled in the chair, buttocks peeled off the vinyl seat, and quickly turned from the window, wrenching her vision away from what might be coming. But she lit a cigarette and clenched it between her teeth, rose, and dared to open an amazingly workable false window enough to reach her hand through.

It was the painting, still bright, work-light lit. How had they done it? She traced the dry, rough texture with her forefinger, and leaned closer into the smell of oil paint until the picture flew apart into shapes and brush strokes of milky gesso and electric pigment. Doris keened backward for a sharper view—sectioned-off by the upper window panes—of the deepest, darkest cerulean blue lake she had ever seen—of the high school and the common, and toward the perimeter of this slightly peculiar place, her own house.

Not her own house.

A much nicer place, she thought, with the wrought iron railing of the widow's walk slate shakes unchipped, and a brilliant sun radiating light off the fresh white clapboards. Really, that much *detail!* Even the whispers of light-starved crab grass under the old willow in the front yard.

(There was no willow in her yard; only a sickly maple sapling and diseased oak.)

She withdrew her hand, backed away from the painting—toward the dinette table— frightened of *seeing*. Her cigarette ash fell to its pristine surface. She blew at it, watched it skitter across the tabletop, into the air and onto the floor. She brushed off the remaining dust with the edge of her hand, and wiped the smear on her dress. Gone.

She took an exhausted drag on her cigarette, the orange ring brightening right down to the pain of her fingertips. She approached the window and cyclorama painting, and thought of grinding the cigarette into the cerulean lake and burning an ashen hole into that relentlessly cheerful sun. She sucked again on the stub until it seared her fingers, oblivious to the cigarette burn, captivated by the blue, blue lake in the picture, and shuffled ever closer, eyes wide-open and unafraid, for a more accurate and expansive stare of an inevitable event she'd yet to fully discover.

***

One steamy summer night, Elaine Simonetti—her perfect jaw, and fierce black eyes, and the pink cud of Bazooka gum between her pearly whites—had asked her best friend (*her ugly sidekick*) Dorrie, if she would go down to the dark lake and sandy beach just off the parking lot. It was safe "as shit," not-to-worry—and just outside the white spill of the mercury and sodium lights and the clouds of gnats and mosquitoes and clacking cicadas. Would she hang on the beach with the other kids? *Would-she-would-she* just stay with her, while Elaine waited to see if Ralph Whitcomb kicked a little sand her way, and she could see what he looked like these days, shirtless, with the lake water and moon on his chest and hairy legs? *(Well, no; why couldn't she just go alone?)*

"Jesus, fuck," said Elaine. Couldn't Doris see—why couldn't she see?—that everyone, all the kids *liked her*? Doris just loathed herself, and it was "Just so fuckin' hard," said Elaine chewing and popping ferociously when Doris had "Dug an enormous hole, got in, clawed the dirt in over her, and hid her beautiful self like "Good-bye cruel world!" when after all, she was only "fuckin' seventeen?"

They drove up in Elaine's brother's shit-box chartreuse convertible—Elaine in her sleek blouse, her nest of shellacked black curls bouncing with the bumps and Doris—just so proud to be with her—enveloped in the chemise of a man's double-X Tee, picking the strands of her windblown red hair from her mouth, heart thudding, no one in memory ever having asked her anywhere.

The pair of them, with rolled blankets and a few beach things, slammed the car doors, clopped through the desolate asphalt parking lot through the edge of white mercury and sodium lights, skirted the insect clouds, to the sandy edge of the town beach. *(And there it was—detailed and layered deep, adjacent to that painted ellipsis of cerulean blue: gritty and water-flattened with the night-smell of lake and decaying leaves.)*

They each took two blanket corners, and when it had billowed down to the sand, Elaine lay down kicking and laughing, delighted with herself and the night and her prospect, while Doris, perplexed and awkward, hunched to her side and fumbled in her carpet bag for her cigarettes and lighter.

You could sprint the planks of the old gray boat dock, cannonball into the lake, swim out past the second set of orange ropes to the platform buoyed-up by empty oil drums, and dive sharply underneath, cutting into the darker water, come up on the other side, and pull your friend in by his dangling leg. You could swing way out on the twisted rope—splinters of hemp cutting into your grasp—away from the mud and water weeds below the highest bank, swing way out and drop off, ball-tucked and wild, and hit the water like a fist. The girls eyed them—those wild show-off boy—and the next one in line for the rope, eager to impress, crouched close and sprang hard within the shrieks and catcalls, leaped to clutch the rope, and blasted the water to ecstatic applause.

Doris watched them—from fifty yards, like skeletal sprites against the moonlit sky. But then one and another neared the diving float, ducked under the orange ropes and rose up again, until both figures, in calf-high water, splashed through to the shore, and to the two crumpled towels Doris had not noticed nearby.

But Elaine must have known.

Ralph Whitcomb approached, otter-like, wet hair slicked to his skull and side-ears sticking out, his new seventeen-year-old muscles straining beneath his skin.

Elaine had left hardly anything to chance: not the strategic placement of their blanket, not the scissor-cross of her legs and plumped-up thighs, not the up-and-down punctuation of her breasts as she shared a world-weary sigh with Doris—as she seemed to only endure the dripping, winded Ralph Whitcomb looming over the two of them. He stretched his towel tight and slack, slack and tight—panted his polite *hello* and nodded to both of them with his quick, round otter's head, and scrutinized them with large filmy eyes, as if they—Elaine and Doris—were equally interesting.

As if.

Could he sit?
"Well, I don't give a fuck," said Elaine.

He crouched; then he sat cross-legged and eager, dripping on Doris and half-soaking the cellophane of her Salems. He stretched his wet legs on their blanket, leaned back on his elbows and called out to his friend Seth, who he'd convinced to come along with him, just as Doris had accompanied Elaine.

Seth Pitts—a stutterer, trapped in early adolescence, odd, unpopular and expendable— stumbled toward them on skinny legs. It was clear Ralph belonged on the blanket with Elaine Simonetti, and Doris belonged somewhere else, but not with anyone in particular.

Doris knew him from around—for years. She knew what he looked like, that he was always eager for something to say—to *her*, it seemed. But gape-mouthed and shy, a grade above her, he slipped by her during fire and atom bomb drills, barely brushed her in the crowded corridors, and nodded apologies for nothing at all. He was more of a *case* than she, but now he had been foisted upon her, skinny and shivering, shoulders cowled with a beach towel, shifting from foot to foot, but just standing there, *waiting*, hiding his shrunken nipples and ribs. He dropped his towel, turned from her, bent to pick up his shirt, and worked it on over his wet arms and chest. Now covered-up and almost assured...

"Did she...? Could she...?" He pointed to a battered aluminium canoe tied to the boat dock, and suggested they get in and go.

"What for?"
"We could, you know..."
"Is that yours?"
"No, but..."
"You think you can just go and borrow it, for f-fuck sake?" *(Elaine's voice from my mouth, my God.)* They walked together *(why not?)* with nothing better to do. She pressed her toes hard into the sand near the boat dock and told him no, she just couldn't, it wasn't theirs. Did he hear her? Didn't he? It wasn't theirs; it isn't *theirs.*

He showed her where to sit.
"No," she said, glaring at him. "Didn't I just *say*--?"
When she had hurt him sufficiently—for being the other half of the two cast-off uglies— when he had turned away, his skinny back, his sharp shoulder blades rising and falling under his damp shirt—she held awkwardly to the thwarts, and heaved herself in. He smiled at her; he stuttered *thank you.* She tested the lake with her finger. He untied the rope at the stern of the borrowed red canoe and, with the blade of his paddle, pushed them off into a long, quiet, liquid glide on the windless lake.

The other boys had gone from the rope swing to dangle their legs off the diving float. Doris knew they had watched her getting into the boat and paddling out, and had tracked her hulking form in silhouette, weighing down the bow, while the boy with skin as pale as his tee, sank his paddle extra deep and pulled back hard, straining his slight arms to move them quickly through the water.

"They're watching me," she said. "Who-?"

"That's why they're so quiet."
"Oh." He saw them, nodded, shrugged one bulb of a shoulder, and pulled a stroke.

"Watching *us,*" he said.
She bit her lower lip, and turned forward. "It's all the same to you," she muttered.

She bent forward and chanced a finger over the gunwale, plunging it down into the cool as if testing the wind. She raked her fingers through the soft waves of water and light that lapped the bow. A crow cawed and echoed in the hollow air; a woman's laugh spiraled skyward from a camp across the lake.

He paddled them out to a beachless cove where scrub grew on stone shelves, and roots of tall, fragrant pines thrust into the cracks of a sheared rock face. He back-paddled them to an easy drift, and held the paddle motionless. She reached out to touch the mottled rock, and stopped the glide. Quiet. Still.

She searched her carpet bag for the damp pack of Salems, looked up at him, held the pack out *(Would he like one--just for argument's sake, why not?)* but she knew he wouldn't, him with his shy smile and turn-away. Her *('fucking'—there was Elaine again)*—her fucking lighter wouldn't work, flint-sparked a weak flame but blew out in a light breeze. She lit-up on her second try, filled her lungs, and sighed out the cloud of smoke on a long, tired wind. The two uglies, she thought—*two uglies.* While on shore, their pretty friends who'd suckered them along for company and adoration—didn't she really know?—were so small: little people, moving into the woods. Just *see* his golden arm and blue-veined neck, her lip gloss and teats—her teeth on him. She saw them oh so clearly as they went deeper through the dark line of trees; she would swear she felt the whole of the warm summer coursing right through them—so envious *(but not really, how could she think that?)* she hardly noticed the slight disturbance in her own reflection.

But then again, she was fat and thin, fat and thin, and then had settled onto the surface of the water as herself (more and less) until the next undulation—when she had stopped imagining her perfect friendship with Elaine, and knew she was at least as large as she'd always been.

Seth turned from the bow, and stared right at her. *(Stuck with him, who can't even talk.)* "Want to say something?" she said. She dared him; Elaine would do that. "Want to say *anything* for chrissake?"
He waited, shrugged, shook his head *no*. "Not really; not right now. Just *quiet*, that's okay."
"I wish..." She thought better of it.
"What?"
She wouldn't answer, but then, "I just wish..."
"You 'just wish...'?"
He irritated her, he really did. "If I *wanted* to say, I *would*."
He turned away.
She paused. "I wish we looked like them." Then said it again. "I wish we looked like them."

Something rocked them. She saw the hand come up wet and quick as a rodent claw, curling around the gunwale, gripping once, pulling hard, and letting go. To port and starboard and stern—pulling and letting go, rocking more and rocking more. Until the hands released, and they—all of them—backed off, treading water, and she saw them clearly—four sewer rat-like heads arranged around the red canoe, four heads and rodent claws—four heads, attached by the neck to this black puddle of a lake.

She muttered, "Sons of bitches."

One spit a piss-stream of water at her; the others laughed. "I know who you are!" tore out of her throat.

They treaded closer. Seth gripped his paddle like a bat. They stopped short with a *Whoa* and a laugh, and came closer again until he hit the hand of one—who cried out enraged, attached himself to the boat with both hands on the gunwale, locked his arms, pulled himself up and pushed the boat down, and urged the others, who grasped at the boat, to rock it and sink it. He grabbed Seth's stick-arm hard, held onto it tight, and pulled him until his bare feet slipped on the boat bottom. Doris shifted to that side too, raw with "Fuckin' bastards! Sons of bitches!" Clumsy with her own awkward weight, the canoe rocked once, scooping into the lake, twice taking on more water, and finally in a great splash bomb, flipped them out into the lake.

Her carpet bag was adrift, seeping the flotsam of her everyday: a Salem pack in cellophane, purse-size Kleenex, a Pay Day candy bar or two, a few Tampax. She salvaged the drenched mess of her sinking wallet, and tore her carpet bag from one of them who swam away to an endless echoing salvo of the worst words and sounds she could conjure. They mocked the two of them and swam, receding in the distance and dark, and soon they were out of range of her ludicrous shaming, her savagery, her fat witch's curses.

***

Doris stared into the painting; she touched her index finger to the leaden sky, the daylight gone, the smudge of an ochre moon, the tepid black lake, with its bloated carp and edge-slime, the smell of water rot.

***

They held to the canoe and swam behind it, kicking it through the water into the cattails, until they righted it, and its bow-half rode up onto the silty mud. She refused his hand, pulled her feet free of shore muck and got in. He tugged the canoe off the bank until it floated, turned toward the open lake and the abandoned diving float, thrust it forward and, with a catch-up vault, he was in with his rescued paddle, driving them forward toward the boat dock.

She had to thank him.
He said he was sorry.
No, she said, it wasn't him.
But *still* he said.
She put one finger in front of her lips.

She only wanted to get dry. She walked the gauntlet of the boat dock quickly, leaving him behind. Was Elaine free now? Still there with her brother's shit-box chartreuse convertible? Could they just pack up and get in and just go—home or somewhere?

(Yes, still there.)

Come out of the woods, languorous and exposed on the beach blanket, they sat up hitching and adjusting Ralph Whitcomb's bathing suit and pushing up a strap that had sloped off Elaine Simonetti's shoulder. They tried not to stare at her; Ralph, suddenly taken with scanning the lake view, and Elaine picking debris from between her toes.

Had Doris dripped on them? Well, no; why would she think--?

She began to gather her things, saying it was late, suggesting that they go—and would Elaine please drive her home? No answer, so again with the words spit out separately, each one perfectly clear for the beautiful morons in front of her.

Would. Elaine. Please. Drive. Her. Home?

She had wished she looked like them and, gifted as she was, she now became the astonished part of them, seeing out at *her:* her torso, shrink-wrapped in soggy cotton cloth, her enormous glandular breasts and dark nipples heavily cradled in the damp white gauze, her belly and naval rotund and pushing out against her wet shirt. She pulled the tee down lower, picked up a towel to hold in front, to shield herself—but stood transfixed by what *they* saw: her arms as large as legs, and her enormous legs ballooning out below her waist, thunderous at her crotch, tapering to her tiny feet. The dewlap of her neck; her wide, generous face—the hurt in her own startled eyes. Her little hands, and the insufficient towel that covered only part of her.

"What?" she asked, knowing what. "Fucking *what*?" she said. And turned. And left.

***

The cigarette burned between her fingers, and smothered the metallic odor of chrome- cleanliness and the studio's bleached floor. It clouded the atmosphere of the painting's day-to- moonlit night (for whatever she saw would come along in time), and the painted town just outside the window, finally changed back and once again had rolled along on someone else's bright vision and charm.

Well then where should she snuff the cigarette out?
In the reflected fuzz-face that bobbed along the formica? Ground into the step-on-a-crack no-wax checkerboard floor?

On the happy house in the painting that was supposed to be her house? On the school?
On the common?
On the lake? Oh on the lake.

She leaned close again into the cool blue pigment—amazing herself. How was she so good at remembering the smallest details of everything?

(Remember these things—and put your school books in your bag, and look close again, before you lock the door and leave.)

The several mile trudge home with the sopping carpet bag. (In the picture, you could almost hop from her happy house to the lake. But no—it was miles to her mother's house.)

The crickets' chirp of sounds made out of insect parts.

The fireflies like crazy asterisks in the hover-mist of a field that bordered the blacktop parking lot.

The cut hay and mauve milkweed flowers; the sweet night air.

Could you ever feel a fox's eyes? Can you hear the worms twisting through the loam?

And oh it hurt, it hurt like everything in this faux happy daylight scene, this fucking lie. (Was it night outside by now?)

And all she wanted (as she reached, with Seth Pitt's outline, mute and *still*, and still distant at the dock, watching her)—all she wanted was to put the cigarette out, dead as it was between her burned fingers—to leave a little evidence she'd been there and knew, just a little ash left in the cool blue waters of the moonlight-lit cerulean lake.

Not so anyone would really notice. (A smudge of gray in the black-and-white. An aberration of texture, if anything. Another false front.)

She gathered her books and put them in her bag, turned off all but the bare work-light, opened the studio door which locked on its own, and left for the city bus-line home.

RICHARD CABUT

ADVERTISING SLOGANS FOR THE FUTURE

Robert peered beyond the colours and was able to make out, not waves like those which had tried to drag him under, but ripples of water. So, that's where they were, by the local canal. In summer darkness, the lighting quality was reminiscent of dusky scenes in some of Peter Greenway's films, especially *Drowning by Numbers* – brim with otherness and the mystical. It was this light which imbued the canal with a sense of romance; enabling it as a conduit of, despite the crap dumped into it, unnatural purity – weaving with the moon reflected on its surface through the margins of something more uncivilised and disorderly. The light and the smell – of shit, piss, blocked drains and something very, very old. The stink took you on a trip and was almost hallucinatory in itself.

He thought, I wonder if I should mention that this it is all a metaphor? He thought this because he was a writer and, unfortunately, writers sometimes have those sort of thoughts: everything is like something else, that's the problem.

Or, at least he thought he might just be a writer. He wrote about music for the NME – although his sights were set on the higher ground, from where you could perhaps see the world and remake it in a way that might be closer to your ever loving/forever hating heart. No one wants to hear about other people's worlds, or dreams – other people's dreams are one of the most boring things, everyone knows that – so the writer, the good writer, is really someone who can manipulate or hoodwink the reader into listening to them talk at length about that strange dream they have just had. So, the writer is a trickster. Robert loved that idea.
If only he had the time, or rather the wherewithal, to write ...
soon...

He thought he might just be a writer because in his head he was always describing, analysing, contextualising, recalibrating experiences and feelings within novelised scenarios – in other words, he could sort of tell a story. He imagined another world and other ways of living.

... in between his preoccupations with the hard grip of the night, the ecstasy (not the drug), dreams of tomorrow – always tomorrow – emotional anarchy, physical chaos, and the twin poles, shrines even, of utter freedom and total security and... nowhereness... Really, though, he knew that writing in your head was not the same as actually writing on paper – putting one, hopefully, beautiful, meaningful, illuminating, not to mention amusing, word in front of the other on paper. Not at all. Even he, in his limited experience, knew that fresh notions, designs and feelings came from the very process of actually writing. The unfolding page itself gave life to new words and worlds. When language isn't written down it is less than zero, Robert thought, maybe there is a God in the typewriter. The Creator. I just tap the keys. I don't know. Who knows? I'm not sure. He infrequently tapped the keys in a meaningful sense in any case.

... this prevarication would continue into old age. Although prevarication is a weird way of looking at writing: when something is ready to be written, it will be.

Robert also felt like a writer because a psychic once told him that he was. The psychic, in Camden Lock, at the top of a row of shops in the courtyard, looked worriedly at Robert. Psychics are usually expert at softening blows when they think they see bad and sad events coming along. They say things like, 'You will be faced with, um, a very challenging situation. You are lucky! You have the chance to grow as person!' This might be in reference to the vision of some profound personal future shock. But Robert's psychic told him straight: 'You have lost track of the arc of your own life. You don't know who you are. You tell and are told lies. You will be very unhappy. You're a writer aren't you? Yes, yes you are, good. The only thing you can do, the only advice I can give you is: don't ever stop writing.'

Robert thought, stop writing? Maybe I should start! But, with the unshakeable youthful (Robert was in his early- twenties) belief in all that is wild and messy, that start would be constantly and consistently postponed. A future deferred. Yes indeed, no time like the future.

But looking at the psychic's tarot cards, a Celtic spread pockmarked by Swords – nine and ten for starters – and listening to the way he told the tale, Robert realised that the best writers are like the best psychics: they can tell the future.

He pondered, in simple terms, writers know what is going to happen at the end of the story – or, if that's the way it is, the creative force of which the writer is an agent knows what's going to happen at the end. And, if writing is a ritual – and most, if not all, writers will tell you that it is – then the process of putting one word after another is nothing if not an invocation.

This thought made even more sense to Robert when he recalled it while he was in the midst of his trip. Bloop!

Still ignoring Marlene, he looked at the water for what seemed like an eternity or more, the way it moved this way and that – swaying murkily; both Robert and the canal.

Robert looked at the canal again and saw the waterway as a ribbon stretching not just from place to place but as some sort of amorphous, unlimited, unstructured time stream – past and future – with ambient undercurrents of subliminal meaning – disorienting but always in motion.

Times flies. But it also flows. This canal, he resolved, is all about time, and being able to see what happens as time, the canal, drifts, cascades and sometimes floods – it is all to do with clairvoyance. If I was a professional psychic, I would set up my stall right here. By the canal side. The canal could be used for scrying in the same way as John Dee's crystal ball.

Robert thought of Derek Jarman's film *Jubilee,* which he had seen several times for the Adam and the Ants footage, and the most truthful depiction of punk of any movie – and never mind Viv Westwood's nonsensical Letter to Derek Jarman T-shirt. More recently he'd realised that the film's real significance lay in the John Dee/alchemy/Ariel/time travel scenes and themes. These sparked in him the idea that life was an array of portents and visions for another, future life. Obviously, no need for acid, this lad. It was this occult chemistry that truly inhabited the film's viewer, in the same way as the film's first piece of music, Brian Eno's ghostly *Slow Water*, from *Music For Films*, which rendered the rest of the soundtrack almost inaudible on a certain level – in this respect it was magic because it made things disappear. Jubilee led Robert to think that even if there is pattern and substance in the universe, this substance is meant to be hallucinatory and arcane. And if it is meant to be chaotic, too, then it also contains a strange acumen which, like the scrying of John Dee, and his like, no one really ever fathoms. Jarman has surpassed himself, he thought – plus, Robert really liked Jordan's twinset and pearls.

Robert loved the sense of possibility in writing (and in fortune telling), but worried that he might sound like one of those earnest academics, or even some of the other writers at the NME who came across like earnest academics – quoting Nietzsche, or whoever, and noting down their brilliant thoughts in their real Filofaxes. Robert only had a fake one. He also read Nietzsche, or whoever, but wouldn't wear it on his sleeve. Paunches, bad breath, receding hair in their youth, these young men – and they were all men – wanted desperately to be regarded as all-knowing but were afraid to catch sight of their reflections in shop windows for fear of disgusting themselves. Looking in the mirror was out of the question. They trembled with fear, Robert had noted, if ever some young woman, in thrall to their clever words, ever approached them. He hated the way they cited Derrida while making it all sound like advertising slogans – they were the sort of who think there's always a simple answer and who can't understand why we can't just... But, Robert thought, the world, as they say, belongs to those who can explain it – and these guys seem as though they are doing just that – they are going to win. They, the fakes and fools, as Robert saw them, are always going to win.

Or, perhaps Robert was feeling a little resentful and jealous – he had come to realise that his career was failing, while theirs' was on the up. No, no, it's not jealousy, he countered his own thought, it's like the fight in the 1950s between the Beatniks and their critics. Those who severely judged their work, their lives.

The Beats were interested in transcendence, the critics only in putting things in dusty boxes. In their tiring search for exactness their lives were half lived. And in their envy, they gave the Beats hell.

Still, a poet can endure anything and everything thrown at him. In response, he or she just writes increasingly miserable poetry. Robert never wanted to be a 'critic' – that was his big problem at the NME.

He thought. If I wrote this story, this very story, about the canal, the acid, Marlene and me, I'd make it, in parts, an unruly stream of babble. But intense. With the liberty to fathom all the forgotten ideas about, maybe, loss of purpose. It would be as much a mood-board as anything, one that would affect the reader as much as something annoyingly posed, depending on the capacity for slo-mo day-glo, or slo-glo day-mo, writing.

He paused.

The action would drift like the swirls in the canal – future and the past. It would definitely need some plot tension though – something that keeps people reading in anticipation. Perhaps.

He peered into those swirls and saw clearly into the future – the canal, he realised, had rendered him clairvoyant. He could now tell the future. Just like that.

Marlene is cheating on me, it's going to get grimy, there will be pain and deliverance, all at once.

It's a true story based on lies, he realised. The most interesting kind of story.

With the idea that we learn a truth, only to try to escape from it. But, in escape there's always both pleasure and pain.
What a drag. There's always a rub and a kick in the teeth, too.
He wondered, is this melodrama enough for people? Ah, readers get too hung up on plot anyway, he said to himself. If nothing happens, everything becomes meaningful.

He continued his acid train of thought: anyway, this story doesn't belong in a book, as such, it needs to be part of an album. Robert had been reading a book of Verlaine's correspondence, and Stéphane Mallarmé, in an 1885 letter to Mr V, mentioned that the bits and pieces he had written over the years, 'Make up an album, but not a book' – which later sparked the imagination of Roland Barthes, who described the idea of the album – circumstantial, discontinuous, and lacking in structure – as a powerful form of expression because it offered what is usually left out.

Robert liked this idea – he thought it might be revelatory and honest. Or, not, perhaps. He could see, decades in the future, talking about this with a pal, Molly, who said, 'Are we lazy for avoiding structures/procedures or are we right in saying the bits that are left out hold all the meaning? Is it an excuse by the writer who doesn't write? Asking for a friend.'

Robert scratched his head and replied, 'I'm still not sure. In any event, imagined books may not turn out as planned in reality, so let's leave it to the God in the typewriter – not to chance, but to the turn of the page. OK?'

Molly nodded her head and shrugged at the same time.
It might need an introduction, Robert thought about this story. A long one. Sometimes a person's life feels like one long introduction – when is it going to properly start? The truth is, sometimes it never does. The introduction will have to suffice.

The thought of it made Robert want to run away.

And if I run away, will the words run with me?

Excerpt from the novel Looking for a Kiss, published by Sweat Drenched Press, November, 2020.

DARK ENTRIES

I dreamed last night I was on a spree
I thought I heard my baby calling me
I got to go, I got to go
I got to go and lose them mean hangover blues

'I'll take you back, baby, if you drink no more'
Gimme my hat and show me the door
I got to go, I got to go
I got to go and lose them mean hangover blues

Mean Hangover Blues
(Jimmie Davis / Buddy Jones)

Ray sits naked on the toilet, gasping. The air is tinctured with the smell of vomit.

A string of spit hangs from his mouth. It threatens – everything is either faintly or overtly threatening in Ray's world – to drop down onto his pubes, an unruly tangle encrusted with dust, static, stasis – and, well, don't ask what else. Really. Don't.

More likely, though, the phlegm will fall onto Ray's little belly, the depository of his beery dreams and schemes, which sags down towards his pubes. A slightly shifting stomach, the contents of which – a lot of beer, some spirits, a few Pringles – had recently been emptied into the toilet bowl above which Ray now sits. He had spewed his guts up.

He hums a tune to himself. A sad, fucked up little dance tune that was being played all over the place recently. Ray probably doesn't know, and it doesn't matter, but the tune is based on an old blues riff. The blues is, of course – goes without saying – a musical genre played by gnarled old American black guys from way back who liked to, had to, share their pain. Ray hasn't heard the blues, after all he's only a tender 24 years of age and it's not exactly his scene, but he knows them. Tales of misery, heartbreak, oppression, waste and regret. Ray lives the blues – mostly the 'waste' part of the equation. And if you were a musicologist, you might be able to make a claim for a specific kind of blues in regard to Ray – the urban blues, a type of refined blues written about the quirks of city life, its lyrics mixing themes of romantic conflict and the good/bad times found within inner-city areas.

This story is an urban blues. A dark urban blues.

All good, hard-hitting blues songs begin with the arresting and immortal line: 'Woke up this morning.'

Woke up this morning and my baby had gone.

Woke up this morning and my money had gone.

Woke up this morning and my baby and my money had both gone.

That kind of thing.

Well, Ray woke up this morning and his baby had gone out somewhere. He woke up this morning and he didn't have any money left after pissing and snorting it away the night before. He woke up this morning with a hangover from the deepest depths. He woke up this morning feeling so bad that he wished he hadn't woke up this morning. He woke up this morning feeling like he always felt when he woke up.

Ray had made it to the toilet just in time. An appealing sight it was not. Readers are lucky to have missed the scene. Ray on all fours, bare arse stuck in the air, on display. Underneath, his balls tight, and small penis flapping, or rather jiggling, with the reverberations of the Richter-scale puking. As Ray heaved into the water, some of it splashed back up onto his face. This made him feel even more sick, great streams gushing at the speed of thought. Or, if not exactly thought – Ray was too fucked to be able to think – then base instinct, at least.

Now, sitting on the toilet, the phlegm falls in slow motion, refracted through it blurrily is a shaft of mid-morning light.

Spit and sick. This is what Ray does best. Or worst, depending on how you might look at it.

At the last moment, Ray groans and leans forward. The string of spit swings out to stretch, break and drop to the tiled floor at his feet. Ray's head tilts down as if in defeat. He looks at the fallen saliva, but it does not register. Then he sees his bare feet. He looks at them for five… ten seconds. A long time. He looks. And wonders to himself:

'How many people notice their own feet? Really notice?'

A teasing, testing question for a young lad to ask himself.

He answers himself vaguely: 'Not many I bet.'

Almost theatrically, Ray opens his eyes wide and stares. He is surprised to find that one of his big toenails is much longer than the other, yellowing, horny, slightly chipped, obviously cut in a haphazard fashion.

The Beat Generation writer William S Burroughs once mentioned that, after taking heroin, he could sit and do nothing but stare at the tip of his shoe for many hours. A complete sense of detachment from the outside world that Ray knows well.

'All those people out there,' Ray continues talking to himself. 'They don't notice their toes. No they don't. But I notice. I notice things because I look. I look because I am a blogger. I observe, and collect details. Then I connect those details to mean something. I can explain what the fucking world is like by describing my toenail.'

Burroughs eat your scrawny, cold heart out.

As if to prove this boast to himself, Ray scrawls roughly in his head: 'When the world is falling apart, there's no place, no space for nice toenails. When the city is in fucking turmoil, there is no time for a pedicure. While everything is so boring, so shit, only the dull fuckers use nail clippers. Nice toenails are for… toerags.'

Ray is pleased. He even feels a little better momentarily – the healing power of creative thought. He especially likes the last line. Who doesn't? But, and this is a crucial but, he knows he will never commit these mental jottings to page – paper or screen. He won't get around to it. With Ray, it's all-internal.

Ray has a blog, but never blogs. He never gets around to it. He can't be bothered. Or, stuff gets in the way – there are other things to get done first. Or, more likely – much more likely, in fact – he's hung over. Sick. Besides, you can't rush into these things. Putting one word in front of another until the page is full, or even half full – is your page half full or half empty? – you have to choose the right words. And that takes time. Longer than the time William Burroughs and Ray spent looking at their respective toenails. Much longer. In fact, until you are sure that any particular sequence of words is the right one, well, better not start at all.

This process of prevarication and pretence is part of the common modern condition. Most of Ray's mates are musicians. But they don't make music. They talk about it, though. They open Mixcloud pages but never make any beats to put on it. They all follow each other's empty pages. If one of them did actually put something up, the others would probably unfollow in shock and jealousy. Or, they are filmmakers who don't film – apart from a bit of homemade porn on the iPad now and again. Or, they are photographers who don't take photos. Ditto. But Ray is a writer. A writer who doesn't write. And we all know what novelist Franz Kafka said about the writer who doesn't write. He is, said Franz, who probably knew all about such matters, 'A monster courting insanity.' Which describes

Ray quite accurately. Although, if Ray were reading these words, he would say, 'Woah, 'monster' is a bit over the fucking top, isn't it?'

Well, let us be that judge of that, Ray, let us be the judge...

In any case, today, the very thought of writing anything at all on his computer is enough to make Ray sick for the second time that morning – multi-hued geysers: reds and purples – the exact colours which would tint his prose, if only he would blog.

Ray's blog is supposed to be about his misadventures in the mean metropolis. But all Ray ever does is go to the pub, or to other people's flats, to drink, smoke and snort. A diet of booze and drugs is the wellspring, or 'unwellspring', if you like, of Ray's lifestyle of doing nothing on an outstanding scale, of floating, monotony and disorder. Most of his time is actually spent recovering. Now, if Ray wrote a blog about hangovers, then he would really be in business.

There is little that Ray does not know about being hung over. He spends much of his time in that raw, sore state. Waking up without a hangover can, as they say, mean only one thing – he is still drunk.

In the good old days hangovers used to be something of an escapade for Ray. They were an experience. Something to be slept through and laughed at later: coping with the shat-in trousers, or the pissed-in pants. The stumbling struggles with dried vomit. The forgetting of friends' names at critical moments, the crazy confusion of misremembering your own name, and the unhappy horror of not being able to recognise members of your family on particularly damaged occasions. Then there's the shock of failing to recall what you really look like in the mirror. Or, the unfortunate inability to forget forever the dark and dumb things said and done in the depths of drunkenness the night before – the unwise, ill-advised and excruciating episodes and utterances that, next day, float to the surface of consciousness like poison filled bubbles, before bursting and revealing their hideous, smelly truths. Blackouts, in this respect, were a blessing. Where Ray was concerned, they weren't some sort of seizure to be scared of.

Rather, the rare successful forgetting of bad shit done the night before.

Sometimes these hangover experiences were merely sad. Occasionally, they were life changing, too.

Ray's mate, Barry, had split from his wife thanks to his stinking hangover. No one bothers getting married these days. What for? It's a hassle. Back in the past, in the dim and distant, people got married young, after they got good jobs, and a nice place to live. Marriage was the final brick in the wall that surrounded a cooing, billing couple with protection, warmth and security from the harsh and unforgiving outside world. But the good jobs and nice places to live don't happen much anymore. At least not to Ray or many of his mates. Any metaphorical wall would be perceived as stultifying, numbing and negating, and would quickly be knocked down. No one got married any more. Except for Barry. Why? Well, he was a retro kind of guy, and felt that marriage would give him some status. People would know him as the 'married bloke.' Many would approach him, inquisitively. He would say to them, before they had even offered the question, 'It's good!' The unasked and pre-empted question being, of course, 'How's married life?' It was good because unlike him, Barry's wife worked, and loved him enough to pay the bills. But the situation, common in this crowd, did not remain good for long. He woke up one morning and his baby left him. In fact, she kicked him out on his arse. Why? Because he killed one of their cats.

Barry, a budding young psycho whose image as a respectable young married was just that, a front, awoke after a night on the lager and weed. He felt like death. That went without saying – if only he could have spoken. Which he couldn't. The state he was in, he could barely grunt. He had retained a sense of smell, though. Which wasn't a good thing as far as Barry was concerned because all he could smell, after drawing up nosefuls of air, was shit. Have I crapped myself again? Barry wondered. His nether regions didn't feel wet and distressed. He put his hand down to check. No. Dry as a bone. Had he experienced a brain tumour? He'd read that people who suffer from such ailments sometimes smell rubber. Perhaps, he puzzled, his own brain is not set at this particular default and, upon tumouring, registers not the stench of rubber, but the stink of fresh turds. That would be fucking typical, Barry thought. He rubbed his head, gave it a little shake. It didn't feel as though his brain had exploded – well, no bigger an explosion than usual after a night out. He opened his eyes. Blinding light. His wife had opened the fucking curtains when she'd gone out. The sadistic bitch. He'd a have a word later. But still, the smell of shit – where was it coming from? He sniffed. Close by! He turned his head on the pillow and came to face to face, or rather nose to turd, with a big pile of shit. Cat shit. The fucking cat, no doubt tired of not being let out, and of not having its tray cleaned, had, in protest, crouched on the pillow next to Barry's sleeping head and voided its bowels. Barry, a blob of shit, on his nose erupted from his pit screaming in anger at the sheer fucking disrespect the cat had shown him. The sheer fucking disregard for Barry's finer feelings. The utter and amazing impudence. The cat, meanwhile, wasn't stupid. It ran, skittering hither and thither, seeking refuge. But Barry was merciless, dislodging the beast from under the bed, and then poking it out from behind the sofa, where it had sought further refuge. Barry finally managed to snag the beast. Terrified, the cat scratched and tore as he held it at arm's length by the scruff of its neck and plunged it into the laundry basket. He closed the lid and watched as the poor animal frantically tried to escape the dark trap. Out of breath, his work done for the moment, Barry rested. He gasped. His beer fumed hangover breath coming short and sharp. Having paused for reflection, he concluded that, all in all, his anger remained undiminished. He opened the laundry basket to exact his revenge. But, taking its chance, the cat, a furry ball of fright, flew out, and ran.

Only twisted bastards pick on dumb animals. His father had once told him this. It didn't stop Barry from approaching the cat where it had tried to find safety – at the bottom of the stairs leading out of the flat. It cowered in dread. Barry moved forward. Slowly. Wide eyed in terror at the approach of its tormentor, the cat noisily evacuated what was left in its bowels. The filth and miasma akin to

Barry's soul. It was the final insult. The last impertinence. Barry crushed the cat's skull, kicking it, stamping on it until the little hallway was slippery with shit, brains and blood. Then, his work finished for the day, Barry went back to bed, carefully avoiding the dead cat's now cold crap on the pillow.

Barry's marriage lasted until his wife came home and slipped over in what was the horrific testament to the murderous power of Barry's hangover. Actually, the marriage lasted until she had cleared the shit from the floor and the pillow, and then she cleaned the shit from her life, too.

Barry later told this story in the pub while having a drink to toast his freedom from the wife. Barry's mates, including Ray, listened. Heads were shaken in response. No one laughed. But no one pointed fingers or blamed. No moral judgement was given. Shit happens. The story, as pub stories always do, had the effect of prompting further hangover tales.

But for Ray, these sorts of hangovers, the ones that you can tell a story about in the pub, are a thing of the past. He has moved on. Progressed. Evolved. Devolved.

Nowadays, drink leaves Ray immobile, oozing sweat and venomous ideas. Booze no longer gives Ray merely a headache; it also cranks up the evil intensity of his thought processes. His hangovers leave him aimless and anxious. The pain felt is not physical, but a mental torment, and a sickness of the soul. In the throes of his hangover, Ray feels a paranoia and guilt so acute that he can do little else but connect and relate to all the badness in the universe, all the shit in the world. Ray feels the horror. He looks at everything, and he does look – he is a blogger after all! – With dead, joyless eyes that are brimming with visions and obsessions from the outskirts – imperceptibles and impulses prowling with ire and the wretched blues. Oh, those blues.

Ray longs for those simple days of innocent, head-holding hangovers that he could laugh off with some Nurofen, a lie-in, and a bit of breakfast. Now, though, his torture is endless. The feelings of panic and distress increasing through the day as if his mind is rotting, allowing the most objectionable and disturbing notions to take a hold. Ray's head bulges with fear, self-recrimination and angst.

In the good old days, the effects of normal hangovers could be alleviated by aforementioned rest and food – and, sometimes, sex. These days, for one reason or another, sex isn't on the agenda. Anyway, the new improved hangover precludes any meaningful link to humanity, of which sex is the most real example. No, with these hangovers, the quality of which is corrosion there is only one thing for Ray to do.

Excerpt from the novel Dark Entries, published by Cold Lips Press, 2019.

GIL DE RAY

VOODOOTRON PART ONE: NUCLEAR SUN

They finally fucking done it. After decades of posturing, sanctions and empty threats. The psychopaths running the planet quit bullshitting and nuked the joint. I watched it all happen. On the internet. It all happened in a night. Bombs dropped everywhere. China got wiped out. Most of Europe too. Africa had nothing to do with any of it but got erased anyway. It was like a video game. I laughed when the news came through that Australia had been destroyed. I don't know why. I've never been there. I just sat there in my one bed basement hovel, far on the edge of town, drinking wine and eating pizza waiting for the end to come.

But the end didn't come. Least not the way I expected. The explosions were terrifying and everything was dark. I barricaded the windows, but it didn't mask the violence or the destruction going on outside. I wrapped myself in my duvet and lay under the bed. Days went by in endless darkness. Black rain pelted through the smashed windows and ran down the walls. The smell of burning toxic waste left a metallic taste in my mouth. I passed in and out of consciousness, waking to note that somehow my hovel looked only marginally worse than usual. The wooden slats I nailed over the windows were dust. Everything inside was soaked. But somehow, I wasn't dead. Apart from coughing up blood, I really didn't feel too bad. When it eventually got light, I crawled through the rubble piled against the window. What I saw outside was unrecognisable in every way possible.

Most of the buildings were destroyed, just gone. The streets made no sense anymore. I'd lived here my whole life and now what I saw was a mystery. The city, in the distance was now submerged, reduced to a massive crater. Where I lived was now high on the edge of the rim of the crater. I watched the remnants of people walking through the rubble, skin hanging off them like shadows. Dead on their feet. The sky was thick, mustard yellow, fires burning everywhere. Acrid smoke hung in the air with the stench of death. Overhead I heard the humming of a drone drifting slowly past. I caught glimpses of it through the fog, a huge black screen, with flashing red lights blinking. A computerised voice boomed:

"STAY CALM, FOLLOW INSTRUCTIONS."

I had no idea what instructions I was supposed to be following. As I walked more drones flew over, blasting a range of high and low frequency tones. My head hurt and my eyes stung with the dust and shit blowing around in the wind. I had no idea where anything was anymore. More people started to appear, and I made sure to keep my distance from them. Everyone was following the drones. I felt an anxious panic rattle inside me. Who was operating these drones? Where were they directing us? What the fuck was happening? I had no choice. I had to find out.

The crater was miles wide, as far as the eye could see in every direction. The high-rise tower blocks and shops and estates were gone, disintegrated. Only the odd crumbled facade peppered the landscape. As I made my descent, I had an uneasy feeling about the whole thing. As more people gathered, an overwhelming feeling of desperation and panic spread. As we got closer, I could see something huge and ominous in the centre of the crater. Hundreds of drones circled the centre. I'd never been to Burning Man festival but this, I thought is what I imagined it to look like. The noise levels rose with every step, the sound blowing wildly around in the wind adding to the weirdness.

People started running towards the stage. Except it wasn't a stage. I didn't know what it was cos I'd never seen anything like it before. Except maybe in a movie. It was a fucking spaceship of some sort. A massive fucking spaceship. Had the aliens finally arrived to emancipate the slaves of the world?

I decided to hang back and let the eager zombies get in there first. I was close enough now to see and I didn't like it. I looked around for somewhere to hide. The skeletal frame of a block of flats. I scrambled into a position where I could see and hear what was going on but not be seen. More drones drifted past, and the people kept coming, seemingly from out of the dust. Hundreds of them. I pulled the duvet tighter. Fixed my hat and cleaned my sunglasses on the driest part of the duvet.

A loud flat sub-bass level tone emanated from the stage. It rumbled through the crowd.

Then a high-pitched squeal signalled something was about to happen.

Lights flashed and in the centre of the stage a massive hologram face appeared. The face of some Aryan youth propaganda movie. Blonde, piercing blue eyes, androgynous and immaculately manicured. The face looked out coldly, flickering in the wind.

'The War is over!' it announced.
The crowd cheered like idiots.
'We are victorious!'

More fucking cheering. What the fuck were they cheering? The accent dripped wealth and an American/English private education. Soulless. Emotionless. "A new world order has been established. The Concordant States Of Earth. As your new leader I aim to bring peace and prosperity back to these ravaged lands. It is imperative for your safety and wellbeing that you follow my instructions and those of the Imperial Concordant Guards, who will provide everyone with a vaccine. This is vital to your survival and will aid in restoring your health and vitality. Do as they say. Dissent will not be tolerated. Failure to comply will result in immediate extermination. Food and temporary shelters will be supplied once the vaccine has been administered. Long live Concordia!"

The hologram flickered and disappeared, replaced by a stream of Imperial Concordant Guards rushing the stage. They looked more like armoured fucking robots to me but that didn't stop the crowd surging forwards to get their vaccine.

I'd seen enough. My head throbbed and my anxiety rocketed inside me. I had to get as far away as possible. Our new masters were holograms and AI robots. Was this really the prize for surviving a Nuclear Apocalypse?

VOODOOTRON PART TWO: WE ARE

I couldn't find my way home. It was dark and bet
avoid drones and zombie people I lost my bearin
the rim of the crater, climbing through the graveyard of burnt-out trees and dilapidated buildings. Hunger was kicking in too. I had to eat something.

Back on the rim, I looked down at the calamity below. Burning Man. Slaves to a Hitler Youth hologram. What the fuck fresh hell was this? Back on relatively flat earth I started to run. As fast and as far as I could. The carnage and debris started to lessen so I guessed I was further out from where I lived, perhaps what used to be the forest. Now more a cemetery of trees. I sat down against the most stable looking tree I could find. Its blackened bark crumbled on touch. My hands gripped the earth. Tears streaked my face. What the fuck now? I looked down at my hands planted in the earth.

Around the base of the tree was an impressive growth of mushrooms. Slimy and long, beautifully hooded mushrooms. Without thinking if they were poisonous or not I snatched them up and shoved them into my mouth greedily. They tasted bad. Bitter. I didn't care. I swallowed them and felt them slowly fill my empty stomach. I had lost count of how many days it had been since I last ate. A lifetime ago. I laughed. Pizza. A fucking mushroom pizza. Garlic. Sourdough. Red wine and pizza. The Apocalypse. What I would give now for a glass of red wine. I looked around the other dead and dying trees and found more mushrooms. Loads of them. Food of the Gods, as Terence said. And he was right. I gathered them all and filled the inside of my duvet with them. I felt like a hero again. And the butterflies in my stomach began to twitch. That old familiar feeling as the rush of psilocybin seeped through my core. I was alive. I was better than alive. More alive than ever. I was not going to die in the crater or become a slave to the robots and the fucking Concordant State of whatever was left. What the fuck was Concordant anyway? Where did they appear

...n? Who were they? And who was the Hitler Youth Love Island reject fronting it?

So, I walked through the darkness, glowing inside as the trees sparked into life pushing me on. The mycelium below the earth radiating love and hope. The sky too, a black sea of death cracked, and a herald appeared, a chariot of light led by an animal-faced being, golden eyed. Showing me the way. A procession of visual delights each more marvellous than the last paraded for me triumphantly, introducing the glory of the galaxy. Geometric shapes, emerald forests, a flowering kaleidoscope pulsing and shifting.

Another figure appeared, shrouded in smoke, exhaling blue gaseous liquid through bull like nostrils. Teaching me how to breathe. It's going to be alright.

There was a presence I couldn't see or hear but I felt it clearly.

You're going to be ok.

And I too became part of the infinite mass and story of the stars. At times, a simple molecule of dust floating in space and then as a huge writhing spiralling multi-dimensional being. I was everything in the cosmos, a god of some sort but not by any conventional understanding of what that meant. An entirely new concept, evolving and changing by the second. Transforming and disintegrating at will. Friendly faces from the aeons of time flashed past me, smiling. Animals, plants and hybrids of both wished me good fortune. I started to cry but the tears were of a happiness I hadn't felt for a very long time. I had the stunning realisation that we as a race of beings are inherently good and pure but have been corrupted from our true nature by our own delusions. What stood in our place was something we were too ashamed to admit to. Or challenge. We were children in a madman's imagination. The evil within us was a part of the natural balance of the universe but we could not accept it and banished those thoughts for fear of upsetting our own egos. That evil was us. Our true nature is the polarity of all these things, the inner self and the outer world. The ego and the will of the universe. We encompass it all.

VOODOOTRON PART THREE: PARIAH

When I woke, I had no recollection of falling asleep, or finding the nest I woke in. As my eyes adjusted to my new surroundings I saw two figures standing in front of me. Dressed in dark robes with face masks, goggles and huge headphones. My first impulse was panic but they motioned for me to stay calm. One of them removed his mask and headphones, "How you doin' man?"

I was totally disorientated. He pointed at the mushrooms scattered around me, smiling. "You look like you're doing real fine. My name's Drago. He's Owsley. You can call him Sly. Whats your name, psychonaut?"

"Uh, I'm not sure anymore."

He laughed, holding his hand out for me to take.

"Ok that's cool, don't worry. None of us use our real names. So just make one up. Man, you smell pretty bad, we need to get you fixed up. Come on, get your shit together. You're coming with us."
As we walked, I felt calm. I had no idea who these guys were or what they wanted with me, but I was happy to be around them. As a rule, I kept myself to myself. I didn't really like people, on the whole I found them unimaginative and dull. As a kid I preferred my own company. And as I got older, I preferred it more and more. I spent most of my time, in my basement. The "cave" I called it. I made music and painted pictures. Drank too much. Smoked weed and occasionally took a dose of mushrooms to keep my mind challenged. I had no real need or desire to communicate with the outside world.

I had a band for a few years, and we travelled together, getting drunk and playing music. That was one of the happiest times I can remember. There's a camaraderie with a band. Like a gang. Playing music with people is as close to having sex without touching that you can get. It's an emotional vulnerability, sharing ideas. But eventually without success the band members drifted away to do other things, join other bands. That hurt for a bit and now that I think of it, I was pretty mean about some of that.

Like being dumped by a girlfriend. I carried the resentment longer than I should have. It damaged me. And people thought I was weird and had overreacted. Which was probably true. I couldn't help it. I couldn't understand it myself. The need for success though was never important to me. The music was all I cared about. And I guess I couldn't understand that for others, the art itself wasn't enough. I guess you could say that I felt like a Pariah. Something about these guys reminded me of the band.

Looking cool, having a purpose. Maybe these guys had a purpose. They looked great in their crazy robes and head gear. Then again, I had a duvet tied round me, so everything is relative, I suppose. It didn't occur to me to ask where we were going or anything like that. I could have been walking into the Hitler youth death camp for all I knew. All I wanted to know was: 'What's with the headphones and masks?'

Sly laughed.

'Man, we'll explain everything when we get to base. It's not just to look cool. It's for protection. From them.'

My eyes followed his hand as he pointed skywards.

'Right.'

In the distance I could see drones buzzing to and from the crater like worker bees returning to the hive.

The full Voodootron album and story is available from WWW.GILDERAY.BANDCAMP.COM

DAVID RUSSELL

FLOOD LADY

How many buildings, how many cities have watery foundations? How many relationships seem to be floating on liquid? Just as some of the buildings in her environs looked, felt shabby and begrimed, so Andrea's relationship with Theodore seemed to have run out of impetus. For a matter of several months now, he was obviously hiding something from her.

"There's someone else, isn't there."

Chester gave a blushing nod.

"Is it anyone I know?"

He remained evasive, "You probably caught a glimpse of her when you visited my workplace."

The penny dropped. There was that one who somehow looked shifty and sinister. Andrea had felt a ripple of hostility tinged with admiration. All became clear.

"I get the picture. What are you looking for? A transitory fling – or does this touch the depths"

His silence spoke volumes.

"Well: it's over between us; I'll leave the path clear for you. I hope it works out."

How many relationships feel like cities in microcosm. Andrea felt the double sensation of liberation and desolation. It was good; it was salvation; but it hurt.

She could not mope and feel sorry for herself – had to recirculate and remedy the situation. So, on to the hairdressers and the outfitters for that truly positive aura. Then on to one of her favourite haunts – an intellectuals' café, with subdued lighting, ideally suited to solitary meditation, intense reading and note-taking for those so inclined; ideally suited to intense dialogue for those in mutually confiding mood.

At first sight, he had the perfect combination of qualities – well-toned ruggedness combined with facial features radiating intellect. His black jacket, shirt, sweater, trousers and shoes faced her dark green corduroy suit, her cream blouse, her black stockings and maroon suede shoes. They looked into each other's eyes, silent, for several minutes. Then, at last, he broke the fast.

> "Hi; I'm Darren. You look interesting."
> "I'm Andrea; so do you."

Conversation was smoothly and swiftly generated.

> "So what's your profession, Andrea?"
> "I'm a research architect. I do surveys for Town Planning authorities. I lecture to people about the histories of cities for various historical associations. And what do you do."
> "I'm an engineer diver. I do maintenance and repair work on underwater installations."

They chatted on about their favourite books and movies, got deeply engrossed, oblivious of time. While they were in the café, the bright day was veiled over; the sky became overcast; be the time they left, it was an inky dark grey. Then came the torrential downpour. They were both rippling, streaming, drenched. But in the great discomfort was a magical frisson. Their mutual magnetism was charged in that savage, chilly torrent.

> "Look; you'd better come to my place, where you can dry out and change."

With something which felt like contrived synchronicity, a taxi pulled up, and they were whisked into shelter. The driver graciously gave them a cloth to dry the seats.

Darren's apartment was spacious, sparsely but tastefully furnished. His lithe, drenched form accelerated her pulse like wildfire. Looking at her, his eyes were appreciative, savouring, but calm. He reached for his chest of drawers, rummaged for a minute or so, then emerged with some unisex underwear, a shirt, sweater and jeans.

> "There; you can go and change in the bathroom."

The bathroom was centrally heated and deliciously comfortable. There was an abundance of thick bath towels. As she stripped and rubbed herself down, she felt as if she were stripping for him, and that the eyes of his imagination were relishing the beautiful spectacle. And it felt as if he were doing the rubbing down. The warm, dry sensation of the change of clothes was so comforting. She returned to the kitchen, bearing her pile of discarded, drenched garments. He was now in a dressing gown.

> "I'll put your clothes in the tumble drier," he said with a smile, taking them from her. She noticed his clothes were already

in the drier – so – anticipation of a wonderful blending. Then he picked up a matching change of clothes. "I'll follow suit," he said.

For the few minutes of his change, she felt like a fantasy voyeur. That body could be a source of universal delight. They went into the sitting room, where there was an ample sofa. Darren played some music on the sound system – subdued, moody progressive jazz.

Darren took a deep breath and looked at her intently. "I was riveted by your lectures; I could keep on replaying them." He drew a deep breath. I hope this isn't being a bit bold and forward to me, but we did have a watery introduction to each other – a sort of Baptism. Could we continue the process?"

How so?"
"Would you like to come diving with me? I'd love to show you round the underwater realm."
Andrea was gobsmacked: "Oh: that would be fabulous!"
"Have you got a wet suit?"
"No; but I've been thinking about getting one for ages. This is just the prompt I needed. Look: I've got to go now; I'll be back in touch when I'm fully equipped."

What a throb of anticipation! Together they had negotiated the malign waters, and now they were to embrace the benign. She knew she had a beach body to match his, but a wet suit would be great for imagination and suspense. She had prevailed against the water's surface; now would conquer its depths. And with such a gorgeous partner.

Long ago, Andrea's grandmother had shown her many films of the underwater expeditions of Hans and Lotte Hass. How long had she had that secret yearning to emulate Lottie. Of course, it would be great to wear a comparable swimsuit, but there could always be future occasions . . .

Her self-preening in the fitting room and before her bedroom mirror turned her fully on. So she would her second degree Baptism – and then.

***

When they reached their rendezvous, the sky was overcast, and there was the suspicion of a chilly breeze. But Andrea now had a thermal wetsuit and surged with confidence. Somehow the greyness of the sky galvanised the allure of the water.

They embraced and kissed before fitting their masks and goggles.

> "I want to carve our names on the base of a submerged pillar, which I can show you."

How the two of them relished their underwater balletics, their flexing bodies counterpointed by the loving swirls of the polychromatic seaweeds, their embraces giving them a sense of the crustacean. So, they plunged to the bed, to the foundation stone of a broken pillar.

There Darren drew a chisel from the zip pocket of his wet suit, and chipped their names, an arrow and a heart. Back into his pocket the chisel; a further embrace, then back to the surface.

They felt a sense of relief, tinged with anticlimax.

> "We'd better go back to my place and dry out our suits."

Once again, the tumble drier did the laps of its sterling, swirling duty. There was a suggestion of steam. Once again, relaxing and chilling out with laid back jazz. Then Darren took a deep breath and looked into Andrea's eyes. "You remember I told you I was enraptured by your lecture. That made my intellect and my libido electrify each other. Please recite it to me now: I'm all eyes and ears, body and mind."

Her hypnotic voice, and the array of data, perfectly relayed through her super-resolution photographic memory, held him in utter thrall. The physicality of the lips gained a perfect fusion with what they were conveying. When her recitation was completed, he felt breathless.

> "I am overwhelmed," he sighed.
> "Henceforth I'll do your every will."

Her eye-contact declared her will with no trace of uncertainty. Now was the time for the third immersion. In some ways, they felt like two bodies of water. The textures of their skins and muscles echoed the scales, fronds and waves. Their embraces and caresses were suffused with a tidal strength. Their falling garments resonated as sand masses and submerged piles; their final melding rotated – a transcendental whirlpool. They made the transcendental eddies and breakers.

***

After their none-too-rapid awakening, they took a leisurely stroll towards the café of their first meeting. Andrea saw, disappearing round the corner, Theodore and his partner – the one she had suspected. They were arm in arm, idyllically happy. She felt so good about them – all venom spent. The two couples became mirrors to each other. Perhaps never a foursome, but very happy.

Excerpt from Pearlman:

Her skill in undoing my armour was worthy of any trained white man. “We are supremely adaptable; we learn avidly from those we observe and oppose”, she whispered, her teeth gleaming in her smile. As I saw the chain mail and the cuirass lying there, discarded, I saw that the rust had all disappeared.

Deft hands tenderly peeled my sweat-ridden leather and cotton; it was lovely to be nursed without immediate wounds to distract from the exquisite sensations.

“You must be proud of your exertions!” she said. The power in her words was akin to a duelling challenge. (The time warp flashed me into my happy collaboration with that beautiful fitness trainer, when I imagined that lithe, toned form excelling itself at the Olympic High Jump as her prelude to our delicious consummation.)

I looked up towards her breasts, to see the matching metal, discs, chains, bangles – an array of gold, silver and jade; I sensed their resilience beneath their cover. She read my response with total ease; with a radiant smile, she whispered “do as you have been done by.”

My hands trembled a little as I delicately negotiated the pins and clasps, but I succeeded in making a harmonious pattern of them, like a crown at the head of my discarded armour. It was good to have gained intimate knowledge of those metallic treasures in the museums.

The face of a full moon, reciprocating its radiation on Tegualda’s face and eyes, beamed its glittering reflections, as if casting off a diaphanous robe, to reveal the perfect body of its illuminated rocks, bouncing back and forth around the elaborated grid of our variegated metalwork – steel, bronze, silver and gold – its luminosity almost suggesting that it would all come to life, radiant

in the flames of their smelting, almost as two armies facing each other. In turn, the beams flooded our faces, giving an external flourish to our luminous vibrancy charged from within.
She took my hand, and made it caress her sealskin robe: "please do the honours". I lifted it at the bottom. My hands reached up inside it until they could feel her firm but still slender waist. Repeating my earlier gesture, she raised her arms in surrender and conquest, the robe clouding into a transient veil over her noble features.

Then Tegualda cast off her gleaming white cotton camisera for me with all the challenging flourish of a toreador. She tamed me and fired me simultaneously with her lovely self-revelation.

The walls of my time-capsule were fractured. There glistened across the world, ricocheted back and forth across the centuries a composite of the world's beauties, celebrated in poetry and song, painting and sculpture, melted, distilled and poured into one vibrant, impassioned, soul-suffused body. Egyptian and Grecian statues and mural figures melted into an array of Hollywood dream sublimities deeply embedded in my memory. This was a spiritual earthquake, embracing all history and culture, the distilled essence of all artistic striving poured into one giant goblet.

JAN WOOLF

THE GREY EYE

The famous painter waits in the wings of the main stage. Nervous. 'I know my stuff, and I'm famous,' he mutters to no one in particular. His interviewer is famous too, what with his yard of books and own TV series. The interviewer was known as passionate, principled. He'd gone on about it in the green room, before saying, 'but we're here to talk about you, Sir Stanley,' the emphasis on the Sir – before genuflecting sarcastically.

'Oh humph,' he'd said, every bit the knighted yet humble painter, 'you'll be offered one in a few years.'

'I like to think I'd turn it…' The famous presenter had swallowed the word 'down' before it could leave his mouth. He'd then gone an interesting pink – flake white mixed with a smear of viridian red. What a study, he'll remember that.

'I have one of your canvases over the mantelpiece at home,' Mr Turn It Down had said.

'Oh? Which one?'

'Er, untitled.'

'What dyer pay for it?' he'd asked, knowing that it was Glad Morning in Uttar Pradesh.

'Thousands.'

An usher comes, a local sixth former, in love with all writers and painters, her hair brushed back, eyes sparkling. Another interesting study, he thinks. Then the presenter is at his elbow, and onto the stage they go, pushing their fame before them, each trying not to trip over the coils of camera wire. They settle to an extended pitter-patter of applause like rain on the canvas walls. Broad smiles beam up at them, sideways smiles, heads cocked, some of them clapping their hands above their heads. A man stands in salute, but no one follows him, so the man sits down, flushed.

Flushed is interesting, he thinks, the red mixed into the white would need to be maroon, the white a Titanium to give it that edge. A hush descends upon the marquee, and he sees the grey eye of the monster. Behind it is its mistress the camerawoman, her hat the wrong way round, tendrils of fair hair escaping. He thinks of Medusa.

'My esteemed guest needs no introduction,' says his interrogator. So, he doesn't get one. He notices a few punters consulting their programmes. Ha! Notices too that all the faces are what old EM Forster called pinko grey. What a good name for a colour, he thinks. They should sell it in tubes.

Studying the diffused light bleeding like tinted steam through the walls, he tries to name its colour. Or is it a hue? He hears the first question loudly, too loudly. Of course, it's the second time of asking.

'So, describe your processes, Sir Stanley.'

'Um,' he replies, and studies the sharp viridian green stain on his own white shoe – a mottled smear from the damp spring grass outside, as smiling fans approached him with pieces of paper for his autograph, a white space at the top for a squiggle, a sketch even. He'd obliged, even though his gallery had asked him not to.

'So,' says Turn it Down. 'the paintings seem spontaneous, not consciously thought about.' He says 'so' at the beginning of each of his sentences.

What twaddle, he thinks, everything is a dance between the Dilly and the Dally, his names for his conscious and unconscious minds. But he says instead.

'No.'

'Oh.'

The crowd grows restless, a few rictus grins, faces fanned by programmes. The eye of the camera is steady, the camerawoman smiling. She doesn't care, he thinks. She just wants her lunch; she's having a laugh. But that grey eye doesn't blink – a milky but opaque grey, an oblong hood around it like a cobra ready to strike at the centre of him. The camerawoman's knee jiggles in her sage green combats.

'Are you comfortable Sir Stanley?' asks Turn It Down, his voice a tad higher.

'Yes!' He doesn't mean to snap but maybe it will release the flow of trapped words. Remove the dam at his tongue. Maybe the words will melt and come trickling out in a sweet flow of art talk, words like voluble, sensual, colour-tension. Some of them slight enough to squeeze through his teeth – bold, thick, thin – or oblong words like motivation, creative processes, non- figurative. Round, plump ones – ellipse, circle, blob. But they clog his mouth, a pallet of unspoken colour straight from the tube, some leaking into turds of white. The words also smell, of linseed oil, turpentine, and fixative. Yet that dull grey eye keeps them locked away. 'So, our time is up,' says Turn It Down. 'Have you anything else to say, Sir Stanley?'

'No,' he says, feeling that the eye might be his friend after all, deciding to ask the camerawoman to lunch to ask her what she saw.

CARLYLE REEDY

THE SOCIAL WORKER'S NARRATIVE

They Call It a City/Night of the Dance

All stops are pulled out here to the South-West. The ripped lamp-post, one of an old style, hangs by a cable. Some hard hand plays with the traffic lights and the bits of building. Inner pieces of the puzzle close in on a man – he becomes one of them. Down as far as the pier there's darkness.

As for getting with it, that's difficult. First must be firmed in the dark a solid obsidian knowledge you keep secret. You have to work through your part of the changes. I say that because I know about it. I call myself the organist. I'm recording a music that's not exactly splendid. I have to hold on to the knowledge and not lose it. I have to include all that's around me. Like my body, this has been used badly. I make the effort to get my sound out about this. It's a struggle in a night that has no sure knowledge of a new sun rising, and it's well into a time that's already ending.

Everywhere in the city men are pretending it hasn't ended. They bow and clap, play with the bodies and bits, the hard and soft pieces. For me, they're dimwits; they've forgotten what I've stored as a hard bitterness. I mean, what was ours has passed into a deathly sleep here. It grows dank and putrid with waiting for a final inhuman touch to put it out. This growing waste has been left by men who've turned away and forgotten it. These terrible neglected vistas of shattered glass and crumbling brick patrolled by dogs were ours.

Sometimes I think I'm alone in the music. I know what it is to be alone in darkness. A thin moon can barely illuminate the pits at the road's edge, the dangerous bleeding holes left where wrecked beams and twisted girders fill with rotted debris. I guess it's just like chess, checkers, Go, drafts. Any simple maths will give an idea of how to get through these places, where to step. You just dodge a few falling tiles of slate and broken brick and you're on: you're doing it, playing the music.

Part of the game is to match bits of rotten building with new blank blocks of insensitized pre-fab materials 'they' give. I don't know 'they's' face – hidden I suppose, behind larger, more ornate oaken doors, solid. I am behind a small door. It rots off its hinges. I pick at it. That's alright, just like in the Middle Ages. I've played this organ before. I'm allowed to be canny like the feudal beggars I guess, to be sly and know my stuff. I can pick a hinge or hammer and fix the mess 'they've' left here. I lurk in the low rangers of the night concerto all right, sniffing and picking like Aggie.

See: what I do is in the prop department. You know about it. I prop up the rotten structure. I bastion a disaster. I'm kept busy. Keeping company with dwarves and mutants is an uneasy task. They turn another colour when you've got your eyes somewhere else – even for an instant. You never know what they're thinking; they're in the pickings too. The leavings round here are meagre for humans. It's alright for dogs though: there are plenty of them, raking the rubbish, howling, scrapping.

In the night you can always see the places I'm heading. It always used to be there, but parts of it got struck. It had been a fantasy once. I'm completely legal: I've got papers to prove my position in the carrion heap, and I'm the one carrying choicest morsels to feed my own. I can just keep the maggots back. Believe me: it is not a simple task; I'm always busy.

Just further into darkness you can see clearly. It's been hit here and there. It was heavily blasted during the war. An old-time inhabitant said people were thrown on the walls and you could see the imprint of the motion, but most were turned to statue in the instant. Just like that – made a picture: frozen action shot. They sell them round here – the old photos, by Johnny's on the corner.

That's the genuine bone, that trade; it's still going. But enough of local colour; I'm getting to the point.

The building I'm in has a rugged up and down frontispiece like a church. It could have been one; then it must have become the factory. You can't tell. No-one has really noted any history, and at present it's hard to find things here. There's a recessed memory, that remnant knowledge, makes of this dump a village once: that's hard to believe. I could believe that up by the cool untroubled squares I'm not walking now, but here where I am there's nothing anyone can tell me I'd be too certain of. No: this place is just a wreck; it's total. Somebody somewhere said I could take over. So one building is as good as another hereabouts; they're all falling. The cheap paint on the outside wall is already peeling; I put it there. It takes a few days and it looks like dirt. Each twist of that paint turning makes my mouth bend like an old orange-skin; it's bitter. The work doesn't get you anywhere, and the taste of charity is enough to make you sick.

Oh, well: this beat-up junkyard is my organ. Given. You don't get any worse, you've got to do something all the same. It's enough to die in – I mean, what else is there?

Someone before I did worked a room into a club here. It was for older boys, for darts. He put cards – there. The alcove was obscure, but he'd planned a library, barring all the supply being nicked. So I cleared a big room for the dance. I left the main structure as it is, shaky. It's a danger, that. I'm always here after I pick at the lock. I stand in a pile of old planks and rotting beams, and I work. The hessian sacks have to be padded over with sponge. They're soggy because no-one could repair the leaks. In the roof. They're open. The water down under the tail skeleton of wood has become stagnant; it's filled with droppings from the rusted iron beams above. Well, it keeps me busy; I repair and mop up.

Like I said, this was a factory once: I can picture that. Two centuries or so of figures trudging in here carrying their loads. The loads would be of coal, concrete and brick, vats of tar and asphalt.

The figures would be in droning patterns of obedient repetitious actions made in time to the machines. The loads would be humps on their backs. Noises accompanying them at their work would be like the long, low unholy moan that is cast overhead – sometimes from planes.

I sanded and lettered the door again. It took an afternoon. I recall feeling the beginnings of this growth of darkness spreading in me; it made my hands sweat – they poured out salt until I felt weak. I had to strain to get hold of anything. The old knowledge was in there but spreading a dark liquid. I figure it as likely I'm just getting old.

The newly fitted door still creaks, horribly. It's frightening. I'm only pretending. Not to be; it's important. It helps everything: it helps that boy John who is coming – not to be afraid of the Alsatians on the corner. Ha: imagine! He and Harry think I'm not afraid. I'm a pretty good actor. It pays, like they say.

No shaft of light from off that street there: that street couldn't send in a shaft even in full day; it's so dismal. Yet John, that boy, is moving – softly. It starts and stops like a leaf falling.

***

He steps elliptically along planking on the side path. Perhaps that lad has a bit of Greek in him; standing there like that, he looks like a statue. Those prehistoric – those Corees – that was it. In Paris, ah! That was back awhile. The smile around those lips when they are actually at rest – it's a very sensual mouth on that statue. The Louvre I think it is. Well, it doesn't matter – but it's curious: that beauty – living – here. He tilts up the small chin; it's formed nicely. He might speak out through this rotten hole we're in. I must be in shadow. He doesn't see me – no: he's not noticing me, crouching in the muck like a peeper. He's moving again, careful on the planks above the filthy water, poised in the stops like an acrobat, balancing. I wonder if he knows what he is – at all; probably no faint notion.

He's stopped again: 'John'? A pure creature – shirt all clean and now pressed. That hair black and curly: maybe Romany. No: the profile is Greek – probably some old auntie and an exotic waiter. Well; it doesn't matter; he didn't see me.

Whatever's there isn't in the others, that's for sure. It's not in Harry; it's not in that dwarfish side-kick Harry carries – that, what's his name, Bruce: that's it. Mean Harry would have a sidekick alright: someone to kick at. Harry's getting sick. 'They' just let that happen; it happens slowly. They leave it to wardens and keepers in this lunatic asylum they call a city to sort it out after it happens, alright. I wonder if it seems to happen slowly or faster when you see it only as a button on a chart. One of those cute red tacks they poke everywhere on the map at the big office. From where 'they' are, they're not sitting over the dying corpses, watching the souls being slowly extinguished. Not like me. 'They' stay safe, up there. Well – to hell with them.

When you stand in a place like here, it's a danger: might hit – the head; you have to keep conscious, watching – always. Get hold of something, to balance in the wreck. Well: I've got a hammer, like they say. I'm not allowed to hit the brats that gang up here. I wouldn't want it – I mean to hit, even if they bait me. I mean, it's the oak door I'd like to get to. I'd rip off the brass with my teeth, than I'd smash it.

Through the stench in this darkness there comes music. Discotheque– I ordered it. Costs heavy, but it's worth it. The dance doesn't happen that often; you have to do it. The older ones get bothered from having nothing to do. They get into trouble; no respect – they haven't been taught it. So, I ordered some records – the stuff they like. There's been a revival; I can feel it, in my bones: the rock.

You'd think it would set the old toes going, but it's a sad vague wave courses through my body. Now: I hear that rock alright. It's mild. Oh well, over the splintered boards that bridge the debris. Get to the door in the murky dark.

That piece of tyre: it rose like a snake. The plank moved under my foot and the black monster crept up – from the pressure. There's a patch on that old abandoned piece of rubber. We are all ruined; and then there is this attempt to repair, but we end up anyway in broken pieces and you can see the patches that made our efforts to get there. The slime in the water could be spittle; it's enough to make you thoroughly sick.

In the dance room all walls have been painted in the cheap colours 'they' allow. I mean the budget makes it that you can't get better. You recognise those colours: they are all institutional, like the hospital or the madhouse or the old people's home – like the lavatories. You get a clean floor in here. By the hand of that old meek dogsbody the Social Worker, you get this planar effect of ultimate bland linoleum and those damned colours. But those benches –well, that was something alright: half a week to fix them, three splinters. I smashed my finger, but I made them look better. They look neat, all lined up.

That boy John again, leaning: his head at an incline like that might be even more beautiful. Vulnerable with the eyes shut; tilted; long lashes and dark. The underside of some soft animal – Oh I don't know. He's just another kid. Is he? Surely. But there's something special about him: none of the others would spread their legs out in that fashion – it's abandoned. When the girls start giggling, he just lays back. Then he starts to stare senselessly at the creases in his pants. It's on him too, the awesome adolescent shyness – maybe because one girl is sad and fat with powdery, lumpish flesh, and the other, in harsh, brash make-up looks almost cruel beneath this hot greenish light in the dance room. Maybe that shyness is only incomprehension. I mean overnight that girl – he probably knew her – painted up her face and shifted into a satin blouse instead of a tee-shirt. Suddenly everything's too tight – the little rock-like breasts start up and the thighs – Oh well: it's their party. Nobody asks what they get up to. You've got to do something.

You would've thought that John would be looking for Harry and Bruce. They come in all loud, expecting everything, and John just gets up like he didn't even see them. He follows in a line I just stroked over to the table. He's – he's imitating me.

At least that's something. He won't ask anything of me though. He just slaps money on the table, hitting the coin flat. He lifts his hand to show the money and takes a fizzy drink. Then he's going to hold it up like a little kid so's I can open it for him. You can't tell if they're children or hard bookies. You can't make it out: it's a twilight area – everything obscure. I mean I've been working at this for a long time here. I couldn't really say I know any one of these people they call adolescent, in this area 'they' call deprived.

Spinning suddenly away – that's startling alright. You wouldn't expect it; how can you expect anything? I don't know. Harry and Bruce get the surprise from him, and then they push too, and john falls about laughing with them. It's chilling: I don't know why, but it is always frightening when they meet. The boys; on the corner; here; for the darts, for the dance. I'm always expecting some disaster from them. It's in the gathering tension in their young forms. They get that expression on their faces and that's the real beginning. But before you get that, you get this nervous apprehension, just in their meeting at all. The worker here before me felt it, but he wasn't afraid. He knew how to work with them. He left notes with me, but it isn't good enough.

Pretty soon their agitation begins; the nervous apprehension has seized their limbs. They start to prance round in front of the girls, trying to attract attention. The girls ignore them; they go on talking and giggling. One of them eats peanuts, smearing the lipstick on her hand and then on her dress. I don't know if I know that one – it's hard to keep track.

That disco – I shouldn't have hired anyone. Someone told me already; I just forget it. Let them run the disco themselves, he said. Makes sense. Look at it; all they want to do is play them. They put their hands everywhere; that annoys the disco chap. They'll get to him; he'll want to leave here. Before that happens, they start closing off. They sit with a callow look – a pouting aggressiveness I've seen before. Through the music you can't make out their words, but the boys are planning something, you can see by their gestures: in a minute, as one mind, they leave here.

Now it's got to be really quick. I have to hurry because that feeling is growing: it's dank, it's fearsome. Quick I step over the debris between the dance room and the office. I have to tell the assistant to oversee the rest. Now out of the sad door I move, called into the night where something evil will stir in the moonlit dark.

Bitterness: The night visits of grey on grey as far as to where Harry and Bruce are walking. Sure to continue for several unearthly meters. Bare wire fences marked with the sign GUARD DOG bastioning wastes of gravel, broken glass, scrap iron. Wire, steel and aluminium measure off everything here. Huge plots of unused land, abandoned into the hiatus created by suspension of a motorway plan. This area is designated as temporary on all the social work papers. Like the lives here. Temporary. Up dog, social worker. Get busy now and control, old boy.

Yeah: the romantic old gas-type lamp, ripped. Beside it the delicacy of architecture like cake crumbling. Cheeses eaten out from within by the poor. Crammed in there like trogs. Our workers, our people, under the whip, shoved in here, and then their families cut up with the old cake. It's disgusting. Somewhere this rotted goody is joined to the pocket of an even more cowardly ageing ponce. That's the rub; you just have to take it. Rubbing in there in the mouldy old pocket with the stale goodies, enough to make you sick.

Now the boys are up by the old bagwash, like the leaves on the trees they gather to turn. When they will be turned, each alone in himself, they will close. Then an even more final change will begin. In the boys, withering happens within. Anyone with eyes can see it on their outside flesh; anybody with ears can hear it coming. The malevolent silence that is here in the night accompanies the death of their innocence.

By dim light they hang, waiting for prey. They'll want Maggie tonight, the old miser. That ragged cat. "She'd sell her mother, she would," the boys had said. "She steals Christmas candles!" Bruce said; but John only watched him. I saw John study the other boy's face. Stupid Bruce would keep an even rhythm in the dull chant. He would be good at baiting the old woman. Maybe stupidity keeps him at it. Surely it is his density that keeps him from remorse. But that boy John is different; even so, I am afraid. It's in the shadows: the shadows are human, or they could have been. What kind of mind lives where the soul-light is so dimmed by indifference? They need to become strong again. How do they meet in the night without arranging it? It is beyond comprehension. The scene upon which I am coming will be too cryptic to figure. One boy will be shut-off, another stupid. I know – what? Hardly anything. Some statistic notation. Will they rush to mock me, in imitation of the demolition experts? Will they stare through the shadow and do nothing to me, but stare with that absent lack of connection which is all they have known from their city fathers? What will they do to me in this darkness? Surely they don't fear it as I do. They are its doom. They are the flowers of this ruin and – as greed and indifference are forcing the demolition of the site of their birth, will they huddle together under the warm street light to comfort each other, and will they turn as one mind suddenly strikes?

My gut is loose as though filled with water. Might shit on the spot. They might shock the old woman Aggie into a hard attack. The cords are inside – there's surely a courage to get hold of. Another notation said 'consciousness of several as one is a phenomenal human ability that in an instance of neglect may be found in the meaning of collective energy as aggression.' Means something: that's how they'll do it then. Just as the old miser emerges from the bagwash, the boys will mass the energy. The energy will mount. It will be up to me to break it somehow. Always now, Aggie creeps out to rifle the dustbins – the old vulture: she's a wretch, bent and twisted like the girders in the ruin. She might be old, but she's skinny and tough. She's ragged, but Harry says she has money stashed beneath a mattress.

Well, this mess is my heavenly organ; I might as well play it. Down to the small black dot that is the old miser's eye, right out through the stinking night that hides what sort of watcher? Is it you? I don't know. People go blind when they don't use their eyes – it's a known fact. Or when there isn't enough light about the place. Wherever those ponces are, behind those oak doors – well, the light must be pure atomic. Why, they can see so far, they can do this to the old bird and the boys by remote control. It's enough to amaze you.

So Aggie, with her head forward on her bent neck, her skinny arms bent to hold the tatty bag for the money she bags by begging, is part of a real scenario – something I've seen: I mean nobody can tell me I didn't, I'm in it. It is a breathing mirey amoebic monster, a growth. It's right on your face like a cancer. And she's in it. I have to gather my guts to enter the pin-point spot on this part of the map alright. I have to stop right in there where jagged Annie is standing curding and screaming at those boys in fear. It's my job. Getting with it. John will pull his shirt up over his head and be in the penombre like a headless ghost. Harry will be circling around Aggie, his arms apishly dangling, a menacing ugly fixity in his glazed eyes and sneering mouth. In the dance an inhuman chuttering alternates with periods of hostile staring silence – something to spin to: just a question of locating in the loose mass of fear just below my belt some sense of purpose. That's hard to find here.

Sad street. In the houses, no-one. Just by the bagwash there's a wooden fence. A light in the window; the old glow. Maybe that one's a left-over, some ageing granny whose family shuffled off to Surbiton. The list is long around here. Maybe those three shadows come up there on the wall behind John, Bruce, Harry and Aggie. Those added on into the night ceremonies are lone cats. Maybe they come out all together out of one of the buildings. More likely they met up in the sterile hallways of the new estate, over a busted ping-pong table. Or maybe they just crept out like rats from one of the buildings as the demolition experts hit it.

For the shady audience Bruce is squirming and cackling, doing flashy shooting out with his arm and getting just behind the old woman. Then he shrieks with laughter when she turns in fear. He and Harry have trapped the old bird more or less between them. Like a creature preyed upon, she's looking wildly for an escape – but everywhere is barred. She couldn't get out then without going through someone; she has to struggle in the middle waving a fist. She's got the other hand clutched firmly in towards her body. It's got the bag in it, that little claw. There's an opening on the edge of the circle. Could step in there, I could. Just get hold of my gut and step to it. Revive the old rhythm. Call up the chant. Get in the pulse of the blood that angry energy, that righteous speech for the bust-up. Impossible: there's no courage, only the beat of my blood increasing. Pounding my ear.

"Come on old girl," Harry is leering, his face dull and his lips slack. "Give us a little; come on dahlin'". But John hangs back. I could step; I could do my little twist, get the bones working in the socket.

Frozen on my time spot, mute, palpitating like a part of a festering sore I like to cure. What's the matter with me? I've studied the problem: it's one thing from a distance; it's different when you're stepping in an oil stain like blood on this shifting street with your knees buckling and a sound like thunder rising in your inner ear.

All at the wall with one face now, set in the hypnotized empty-eyed effort to call up the energy to strike. John with his shirt over his head, moving and fluttering. The boys on the sideline hang in towards Bruce and Harry, adopting each the simian pose of menace – classical, and typical of the night dance. Aggie screams, drawing dirty creases down from her mouth like running cuts. Flapping her tattered black coat at Harry she spins, like a ball of tangled hair in the darkness. In this mess there is a human face – twisted, the narrow mole eyes squeeze up as though she will cry or vomit. I was just about to leap when something hit.

It was John. His back was so straight, his chin held up, lifted in the tint that gives to his face this archaic nobility. The even profile, like on a coin of gold, is lit by the light of the old gas lamp. He just grabbed Harry's arm and held it back. I saw Harry turn in anger, trying to shake him off. I saw how Harry was weak finally; my gut fell into place. I tightened the cords in there and stepped into my place.

A police car, called maybe by the granny with the wooden fence, slides up. Shadows on the wall detach and flee. In the barren street, there is an echo of the heels as they run. Bruce got away, but John would not let go of Harry. Hard against john's hand, Harry was pushing. Standing in front of Aggie I could hear whining – she, going to squeeze some tears for the police to show how she's been wronged. The old bitch is tough. Under the sooty grime her eyes are watching; she moans and whinges like a cur. She's anticipating being petted by the saviours. Fat with the same deception and cowardice I too am standing, a part of the sore finally. There isn't anything in me to make a difference between me and this place of pure despair. There has been no heroic, only the loose flop of my ungirded gut. I couldn't find a footing on the slick street when it mattered. No: it was my turn. And I missed it altogether. Good I should stand with the whining old women.

"I don't expect you boys to have any sympathy," I announce emptily to the staring street, but John has finally been hit by Harry. Yes: Harry shook off John's hand in an upward thrust, grazing the uplifted chin, and John fell – into the arms of a waiting policeman. Nice: being steered towards the car, soon to be utterly lost in the darkness. My mouth is working, and inside I'm babbling a flood of hot blood, near boiling. I'll be sick here finally; I've felt it coming. Should be big vomit. Surely it will form a word – like careful – be careful of that boy; he's sensitive, special – something like that. I wipe off the spittle and make the try. But my hand is shaking, my whole arm. My gut is trembling like a loose hot water bottle. Middle-aged and useless this body is, part of the mess. Inept and mute, I struggle forward, but the policeman is pushing John gently towards the car. John's beautiful face is strange; a sound that is guttural and ugly, like the liquid in my belly, fights in the alabaster smoothness of his young throat. Then, you know, just before John stooped to enter the car, he threw it. "You stupid fuckin' social worker idiot!" It was the puke of despair I felt within me. John had hardened it in himself and he had thrown it as a stone.

Oh I'm alive alright; the appellation was just. I call myself the organist, though, because that's not all there is to it. No: I'm alive – maybe not quite on time, but as for the dance – well: I can swing it. There: where the beat is in the veins of a man who knows time is ending. In the moment the knowledge of death comes, where menace suspends, the blow is never struck. The annihilation of innocence is barely prevented. I'm living. A heavy, thwarted form. I am propped like a dummy on the scene of a crime. Love is not dead in me; it has taken form in the darkness as despair; it is held back by fear. But still it pulses energy; I grab the cords and tighten. Before the darkness shuts entirely on the fair form of the boy John with his Greek profile and his gentle smile, I will plunge, quickly from the rim edge of faltering light, to save – something. I am dank and shapeless, with loose sweating flesh, flurried and disorganised in waves of eagerness. I see a flash of mother-form in me, of father holding something white and plain. I am afraid; my sweat feels like blood. Yet I leap at the last for the dance before all finishes.

So all the cards 'they' gave add up to something. Those explanations, lengthy and verbose, the ornate addenda of a civil sense of duty; those are some of the final chords on the organ. It's a bad joke: you make a noise loud enough and a door will always open from the inside. I can stuff the tatty cards back into a side pocket. Thanking the police, I say the hell with everyone and hold the door open on the rising figure of the boy. At last, when I am sure he has escaped for the moment the complex trap that has been so carefully laid for him, I relax. It's horrible: I am a trembling wreck of juddering flesh, jaw hanging slack, my tongue sagging, wet all over with the sweat I've poured. The street is silent. In the lamplight John stands, breathing coolly. It's September; the leaves are just about to turn.

I guess that's it for now: the music's played; I'm exhausted – truly. You know the feeling. You just walk back. Maybe by the river, in the same strange scene. You take the kid with you: it's a job like any other. You have to watch out for piles of broken iron, pits between the street and the buildings. You can never tell, anything. Still I wouldn't mind having been able to say just one thing – bright and fair like his face. I couldn't find a word. I just put the stops back in slowly – like this, walking – back through the abandoned scenario of glass, broken brick and tin. But I would have liked to say something like 'son', or maybe 'Johnnie me lad'; I guess it would have sounded lonely.

Postscript to the Social worker's Narrative

Now I hear that rock, alright. It's mild. The room's fetid order has a poisonous quality. On parts of the beams and the falling plaster great funguses spread. You can pick them off with your fingers, exhilarated in the dread you feel about what their gases may be doing to your brain, wondering at the stains they leave on your fingers. It's all part of the work I do; after a while a man can get good at anything. There's more to it, but I'll explain later. At the moment, listening to the music, I am wondering why a man stood up today in front of an empty building and declaimed a kind of violent epitaph on the backs of two people – two men and a woman, leaving the place.

It was impossible at that time, just before twilight, to tell if the four of them had all lived together in the building. The building was like this one. I figured the three passing as unwashed, and even though the stone talc from the stumbling concrete had been brushed off their coats, I figured from the stench they had a hard time bathing. Most of the pipes in these places have been ripped – for the copper, maybe. Some of the residential buildings were old. Picturesque, lonely and blind-eyed they stand everywhere I pass these days. I cannot know whether they are part of a bad dream I have entered unknowingly – or whether in fact this is reality, and all has changed so swiftly I have not been able to keep up. In any case, without company it is impossible to find out. From the position of loneliness I am in I could tell very little about those persons. It looked to me, of course, that they were playing their part easily, as though they knew how to exist in such conditions. The house behind them had been torn up, and its guts were hanging out the downstairs windows. Apparently, the upstairs was habitable, because the man who delivered the speech was praising the safety and sanitary conditions he had created upstairs – only to have them usurped by the departing threesome, who possessed a key to the place and had apparently locked him out. The condemnation he hurled on their backs, coupled with the shadowy figures as they slunk from him, this passing in a starless dark beneath the awesome solidity of the power station, the only remaining official building – made of the scene a terrible spectacle which had about it something of a diabolical finality. Imprecations caught by the winter, which hurtled down the miserable street, bouncing their reverberations off the occult-patterned manholes that line that road. It's the road that leads here, to the place I'm in.

VAL VASSAY

ROBOT RULE?

I was so happy. We'd got married a few days before on the island of Barra in the Outer Hebrides. We'd spent the first night of our honeymoon there then flown to Glasgow for the second night, before flying to Miami. Now, here we were in "La Serenissima", a beautiful, Art Deco hotel on South Beach.

Our ocean-facing room was huge with a super king size bed and a luxurious bathroom with sunken bath – a big step-up from our tiny flat in Glasgow. We were still unpacking when there was a knock at the door. It was the Duty Manager, accompanied by a stunning young woman.

"May we come in for a moment, please?" he asked.
"Yes, of course," I said.

Once inside he said: "This is Ruby, your maid. She'll look after you throughout your stay. Anything you need, just press the red button on the phone and Ruby will come running."
"That sounds wonderful but we didn't ask for a maid and I don't think we can afford one," I said.
"Ruby's part of the wedding package. You don't have to pay extra for her, so don't worry. By the way, she's a robot – aren't you, Ruby? She's our first robot maid. If she proves more efficient than our human maids we'll employ more robots. See how it goes. Any problems, just ring Reception. So, enjoy Ruby and your honeymoon. 'Bye for now."

He left Ruby with us. She was gorgeous: blonde hair in a tiny bun on top of her head; enormous, blue eyes matching the colour of the scarf round her neck; high cheek bones and a kissable pink mouth. Mike couldn't take his eyes off her but eventually said:
"Hullo, Ruby. You're a lovely surprise. Never had a maid before, let alone a robot maid. Good to have you around."

"Good to be here, Mike. Anything you need, just press the button."

"I'm not sure I want her around, Mike," I said, once she´d left. "I mean, she´s a robot!"

"It'll be great. We'll get her to bring us full Scottish breakfast in bed every morning, polish my shoes, whatever! I've been looking for someone like her all my life."

I wanted to slap him!

***

We loved Miami: the sea, the shops, the sunshine. As our honeymoon went on we began to dread going home, but we'd have to go back to work, of course. We'd miss almost everything about Miami, although I wouldn´t miss Ruby, who was getting on my nerves more and more. She was always around. Every time I turned my head, there she was. She talked a lot to Mike, almost ignored me. I told Mike I'd rather not have her popping in whenever she felt like it, but he said I was paranoid, that she only came when he asked her to.

I didn't like the sound of that and wondered if he'd been calling her when I was at the hairdressers or having a look round the shops. I asked him - but he denied it. He would, wouldn't he? He's a man – he's not going to confess to anything unless he absolutely has to.

Still, we were having such a lovely time, it seemed churlish to argue about Ruby or anything else. Maybe Mike was right. Maybe I was paranoid. I must admit I didn't like other women looking at Mike – which many did as he was a handsome chap.

On our last day, Mike had gone to Reception to settle the bill while I finished packing, when the door opened and in walked Ruby.

"Hullo. What're you doing here? I didn't call you."

She didn't answer. Just walked over, punched me in the face, grabbed my hair and started hauling me towards the bathroom, yelling:

"I want him! I love him! Why should you have such a lovely man when I've got nobody? You don't deserve him. I'm taking him."
"Stop it, Ruby," I screamed. "You're a bloody robot - how can you have a man? You're not human. Let go of me!"

She didn't – kept dragging me ever nearer the bathroom. I struggled frantically to escape but she was strong and I couldn't shake her off. Suddenly she collapsed on top of me and I managed to crawl out from under her. Mike was standing there. He helped me up and held me tight – I was shaking.

"She must've gone mad. Marched in and attacked me. Said she loved you and was going to have you. I'm sure she meant to drown me. Good job you came when you did or I'd be dead by now. How did you get her to stop?"
Mike laughed: "You know that scarf she always wore round her neck?"
"Ye-es."
"Well, it was hiding the on/off switch. I switched her off. Simple."

FUNNY HOW LIFE TURNS OUT

"Jean?" said the tall, tired-looking woman who'd stopped in front of me on the High Street of my home town. I hadn't been home for years and had no idea who the woman was.

"Ye-es," I answered.

"I'd know you anywhere, Jean, even after all these years. How's life treating you?"

"Fine, thanks. Yourself?" I said, thinking that by the look of her, life hadn't been kind.

"Oh, so-so. Could be better, could be worse, but mustn't complain."

I tried to think who she was but finally had to say:

"I'm sorry, but I don't remember you. Were we at school together, or did we work together at some stage? I can't place you."

"I'm Gloria! Remember? We were best friends at Brucefield Primary School for a while! Used to do everything together – most things anyway."

It started to come back to me: the pretty, blonde girl who lived along the road from us. She was an only child. Her mother worked in the dress shop in town, while her father worked in the offices of the National Coal Board, not "down the pit" like everyone else's Dad in our housing scheme.

"Oh, I remember now. We used to walk home from school together and I often came to your house to play until your Mum got back from work."

"That's right. We had fun, didn't we, even though we were so different?"

"Yes, we did."

Then a long-forgotten memory came back to me:

"But I must admit I was jealous of you sometimes: for being an only child, while I was the oldest of my parents' five children; and for modelling children's clothes when your Mum's dress shop had fashion shows." Gloria laughed, "Fancy remembering that, after all these years."

"How could I forget? The shop gave you a present of one of the fur coats you´d modelled, and that summer your Mum bought you a pair of silver sandals for your holiday in Italy. I´d never seen anything as beautiful as that fur coat and those silver sandals. It's funny now but at the time I was desolate. I couldn´t see me ever having any beautiful things, or going to Italy or anywhere else. Funny how life turns out, isn´t it? I´ve been all over the world since then."

"Lucky you! Fancy popping in here for coffee? It´s a bit chilly this morning?"

I didn´t really have time to spend with Gloria – I had a lot to do that day - but decided that as I hadn´t seen her for about 30 years and would probably never see her again, I´d make time.

"OK. I´m meeting my husband in about half-an-hour but we can have a quick cuppa."

***

By the time I left that café I felt as if I´d been dragged out of my comfort zone by the hair. I wished I hadn´t met her again, wished I hadn´t stopped for coffee, wished she´d kept her life story to herself.

I thought the waitress gave Gloria a funny look when we walked in, but she didn´t say anything, not even "Good morning". It was only when the coffees arrived that I noticed Gloria was shaking so badly she could hardly lift her cup to her mouth. Neither of us mentioned this and Gloria began telling me about her life since she last saw me.

It was a horror story! She´d had a nervous breakdown at the age of thirteen, brought on by her mother´s over-strictness and terrifying rages. When Gloria´s silver sandals went missing before they went to Italy her mother had gone berserk and beaten her with a belt; Gloria had had to be admitted to a psychiatric hospital. On her release months later she´d taken to drugs, drink, stealing and deviant men, one of whom she married as soon as she was sixteen and ran away from a year later when his beatings got too much to take.

At the end of this sorry tale Gloria asked if I could spare her some change. I didn´t ask what she would spend it on, just gave her 50 pounds, wished her well and raced out the door, never looking back.

I´ve never been so glad to see my husband as I was ten minutes later when I met him for lunch. But I´ve always been glad to see him, ever since he arrested me for being drunk and disorderly and smashing the windows of that shoe shop on Glasgow´s Sauchiehall Street many years ago - I never could resist beautiful shoes. Drunk as I was at the time, I realised that here was the man who would be my rock, who would save me from self-destruction. I´ve been a sober, law-abiding citizen ever since – but I've always felt guilty about stealing Gloria´s silver sandals.

GAVIN MCGARVEY

THE NUMBERS GAME

It had always been the numbers. The numbers had driven everything. They had given him power and now it seemed they were going to take his life. He struggled for air, struggled to stay near the surface as the sea relentlessly dragged him down.

The suit he was wearing didn't make it any easier. At first, he'd objected when his advisers suggested he wear it, but then he'd seen the polling they'd done. Keeping the suit on would make him look like a man of action, serious, brave; they said it would give him an extra 10% bump in the polls.

And he needed it. He had been the lowest polling prime minister since records began for months now. He had to do something about it. The polls showed that the public that had once loved him so, now reviled him. Where once he a sensitive listener, now he was a conniving opportunist. Where once his carefully chosen positions were interpreted as strong principles, now they were viewed as vote hungry posturing.

As someone for whom the polls had been their guiding light throughout their long career in politics, he knew better than to ignore them. How else could he lead the public if he didn't know where they were going?

And that's when it was suggested. Who could fail to love a man who had risked his own life to save another?

It had even been the focus group that had chosen the method. Saving his wife from drowning was, according to public opinion, the most heroic act he could feasibly fake. They'd road tested everything from burning buildings to plane crashes, but it was a drowning the public wanted, so it was a drowning they would get.

He'd always been the man who'd given the public what they wanted. Who else could have brought back hanging? Gotten rid of the immigrants? Come down like a ton of bricks on benefit scrounging dole bludgers? Re-instated corporal punishment so that the young could learn some respect? Put criminals away for longer? Yes, he had a record that you could be proud of.

Still, it hadn't helped. For some reason, it had been difficult to make things stick. Whenever he'd defeated one of their enemies for them, another would appear. Immigrants gone, what about the benefit scroungers? Benefits gone, what about the old, the disabled, the young? Sadly, no matter how far he'd tried, he'd never been able to keep up with their insatiable demand for victims.

And now it seemed as if he was to be their victim. Here he was fighting for his life, all on film, all for the delectation of the great unwashed. As he slowly slipped beneath the waves, he could feel his poll numbers rising. The crash of the waves and the roar of the helicopter above made thinking difficult. He didn't know how much longer he could last. It wasn't supposed to be like this. This wasn't what he'd planned.

It must have only been five minutes since they'd hoisted his wife to safety, but if felt like five hours. Why hadn't they picked him up too? He could feel the wind rising, feel the waves getting stronger. She hadn't known about it of course, the plan. No, he couldn't trust her that far. Her surprise when she'd fallen into the sea was genuine. She didn't even notice the helping hand she'd been given.

When the plan had been proposed, someone questioned whether he didn't think it too big a risk to put my wife into the water with me. He just looked at them. "Like I told the people on benefits, it's either sink or swim". It had gotten a good laugh from his advisors.

How he regretted those words now.

And then it happened. He knew not how it happened. The helicopter flew away. Taking with it his last chance of survival. Not just physically, but worse than that politically. What was the point of a heroic death if nobody saw it?

He was wrong though. Indeed, whenever there was a poll of dead politicians, he always came top.

THE HUNT

It didn't seem right to hunt humans when we didn't need to eat the meat.

Centuries ago, we needed to hunt them to survive, had risked starvation if we were unable to feast on their flesh. Yet now it continued only in the name of tradition. And a tradition that I couldn't help but see as anything other than cruel.

Of course, there were still a few among us who ate their flesh, or adorned themselves with trinkets made using their skin and bones, but for most of us the humans were now merely objects of pity, driven from their cities to the most extreme of climates, or put up for display in Zoos.

Yet despite the decrease in their numbers, still the hunts continued. To some, it was a rite of passage, your first kill. Taking pride in the death of a defenceless animal? It filled me with revulsion.

There were even some of us who justified the hunts by saying that humans had no feelings. How could it be wrong to kill a creature without a soul?

Mostly, this was based on their behaviour when they were our rulers. The building of factories of death, the devouring of other living creatures without a thought to the life they had taken, I shuddered to think of what I learnt of them in my history lessons. But no. I could not agree. Their shrieks of fear when we surrounded them. The way that a female human would charge against all odds in the futile hope of saving one of their young. No, they certainly had feeling for their own; they only lacked feeling for those that were different to them. In fact, their indifference had resulted in our own saying, "Cruel as a human".

Myself, I would not have been here if it hadn't been for my father, and my need, my need to please him, to be the good son, to be more like him. Still, despite whatever cruelties the humans had inflicted on us, I could never sink so low as to take one of their lives I told myself. They were nearly extinct after all. I would come along I said, but I would not partake in their slaughter.

The howl of the horn woke me from my musings.

In the distance, I could see movement How many were there? Three? Four? The thrill of the chase galvanised us, and the fire of excitement seemed to dance between us as we increased our pace. Soon we would be upon them. There would be no mercy.

Ahead of us, the beaters had managed to flush a family out of their cave. The humans spilled out of their hole disorientated by the noise and smoke that had been used to drive them out.

As we bore down on them, the adult male charged us his face torn between hatred and fear. In a moment, all my principles were gone, and I was upon him going straight at his throat. An ancient desire had taken over me. My actions were not my own. Lost in bloodthirsty delight, I struggled to regain control of my actions until finally, as my shame overcame my passion, I pulled myself away from his corpse.

The horn blew again, and I looked up.

The rest of the family, a female and two children, one an infant, were trying to escape. My bloodlust sated I had no desire now to kill. Still, having culled the male, I had no choice but to dispatch the rest. Human society was notoriously fragmented; no other tribe would take them in. They would not last the winter. Killing them now was kinder than letting them starve.

We moved in for the kill. It was an act of mercy.

COMMUNITY SPIRIT

Lined with three-bedroom terraced houses, it was much the same as any street that you might find in a provincial town. What first drew my attention to it, however, was the incredible community spirit of the residents. It was remarkable.

It was during the summer of 2020 and the Coronavirus crisis had hit the country hard. For the VE day celebrations, the whole of the street was blocked off for a street party. It even brought people along like me, curious outsiders, who lived nearby and heard the music and were drawn in by the laughter, to come and see.

Although nothing was said, you could sense there was an awkwardness at someone not from the street in their midst, and I retired to watch them at a distance from my desk in an adjoining and sadly less festive road.

As I watched, over the course of the sunny afternoon, I could see the social distancing breaking down, until by the end they were dancing in the road. Even the killer virus it seemed was unable to keep apart these kindred spirits.

That made it all the stranger when the murders started, an invisible killer that was unfortunately all too human. It even made the national news for a while as you will probably have read.

Surprisingly, the first murder didn't really register much in the way of shock, in fact there was more of a collective shrug at the rather grisly fate of Mr Andrews from number 114. There had, it was felt, been something slightly condescending in his tone. A teacher, by profession, he was pushing forty and still unmarried. Even when he came out to clap for the NHS, he still felt something of an outsider to the families and old folk that lined the street.

When he brought out his "Banging for Boris" banner, there had been a brief warming to him, but it didn't last. There was something altogether too cynical in his eye, too louche in his manner, and the can of craft beer in his hand sat uncomfortably with the family values that the street clung onto so dearly. His beard didn't help. The fact that he had been smothered with the cloth from this very banner had seemed to some like a poetic justice for someone perhaps a little too clever for the people he lived next-door to.

It was only after the next death that the street really woke up to the fact there was a killer amongst them. That was when all the trouble really started.

Mrs Wight in many ways seemed to fit in seamlessly with the other families, being both married and having three teenage children.

Most people were even prepared to overlook the fact that her husband was French as long as he didn't speak his native tongue in public. Somehow the papers got hold of the fact that she had been poisoned, and despite the mounting evidence of a killer among them, her neighbours wondered whether her husband, not really being one of them, might even have done it. They had been heard arguing after all.

While two could conceivably be a coincidence, when Miss Wilkin's body turned up with a cake knife stuck in her back, the truth could be avoided no longer. She had been the embodiment, in some ways, of what community spirit was. She baked cakes and raised money for all sorts of charities. Forever collecting money for one good cause or another, she had played a key role in organising the foodbank collections whilst clapping for the NHS. Yes, now one of their own had been killed things had definitively taken a turn for the worse.

From there, an atmosphere of mistrust developed as the press descended to try and find the reason behind this string of senseless slaughter. Neighbour turned on neighbour. Everyone was a suspect.

It was in this search for a culprit that Ray Slater came to the forefront. Nobody was more vocal about the need for us all to stick together in this time of crisis than Ray. He was of course well known to all the residents of the street. He even made a point of bringing a welcome basket to everyone when they first arrived, and invited them to join in everything from his poker night to the quiz down the local pub.

It was Ray who led the street's own investigation into the deaths. As he pointed out, there was no point in cooperating with the police, who were clearly trying to divide them.

Somehow this investigation led a committee of concerned citizens to the door of old Mr Beswick. If Ray embodied community spirit, Mr Beswick was its antithesis. A veteran of the second world war and a widower, he was a man who kept himself to himself, suspiciously so. He'd even refused to join in the VE day celebrations lacking even the grace to explain himself.

What started out with polite questions, quickly descended into sharp words, and then pushing and shoving. How the fire got started, even now, isn't clear, but it spread as quickly as it started. And, with Mr Beswick lying unconscious on his living room carpet, flames seemed to dance across the roofs.

By the time, the old man had been dragged out, there was a roar of flames up ahead, and his neighbours were spilling out of their houses fear etched upon their faces. Ugly looks were thrown in the direction of Mr Beswick, and it's difficult to tell what might have happened if the fire brigade hadn't turned up to inadvertently reveal the truth.

It was while trying to find a fire hydrant that they had to break into Ray's house. And there it was, all laid out: pictures of the victims, the tools of the murderer's trade, and the poison.

When the police came to drag him away, there was a sadness that came over the street. I came out to witness it myself ignoring the looks I got. His spluttering rage spilled out a stream of bile against the smart arses, foreigners, and do-gooders. It seemed that more was lost that day than bricks and mortar. Their community spirit was diminished.

Ray got ten years for it in the end, something to do with a lack of evidence, but he only did five. No one from the street attended the funeral of Old Mr Beswick, but when Ray got out, they celebrated like it was VE day.

GEOFF SAUNDERS

WHERE IS DOREEN?

'Where is Doreen?'

'Oh, OK, give her five minutes. But answer me this – no, to the left, Raj, otherwise you can't see the door – answer me this: why does Doreen have a "choking fit" at the same point in every rehearsal?'

'Because it's three rehearsals running. We get to "Let me explain, Parkin," and she's off, choking. If the character was choking, I'd think Doreen was going all Method on us, but, no, the character is about to embark on a two-page speech, um, explaining to Parkin …'

'Yes, it had occurred to me that she hasn't learned the lines, but why doesn't she just say so?'

'Oh, OK, we'll go from the end of her speech to "give her time to recover". Oh, look at my naughty fingers, involuntarily doing air quotes …'

'No, Parkin doesn't cry in this scene, Ryland. She's just told him she's leaving Rinaldo, the Italian stallion, to return to him, but she cries, he doesn't …'

'Because he is English and repressed. Remember, we discussed that? At length.'

'Yes, your weeping in The Browning Version was mentioned in the Gazette, but you don't have to cry in every show.'

'Was it quite appropriate in Cinderella …?'

'Parkin doesn't cry.'

'Ever.'

'Excuse me … Red carnations? Really? This is Cap Ferrat, not Croydon … Yes, well, if you'd planned ahead we could have had prop flowers from a professional supplier, not something borrowed from the crematorium …'

'Right! Act Two Scene 3. From the end of Gianetta's two-page speech, the one I am hoping to rehearse at some stage before the dress …'

'Ryland, you're by the piano, thank you, and Stella … where is Stella?

'There you are. Please try to stay awake, Stella …'
'Yes, I know it's been a long rehearsal. And it hasn't even started!'
'Are we all set?'
'OK?'
'Good. And … action!'
'And … curtain!'
'Thank you, everyone, that was … Better. Though I am glad we still have a few more rehearsals …'
'Yes, Ryland, it's coming along.'
'That's true. I just think that when you are listening rather than talking, you could maybe do … a bit less. Stella was doing her big speech (after a fashion) and you looked like you were simultaneously prizing a toffee off your molars and trying to shift some wind.'
'Just … listen. It's her moment.'
'Parkin is one of the main characters, yes, and yes, your turn in King Lear may well have gained us some extra audience members (who can forget Edmund the Bastard played as a predatory homosexual in a leather harness?) but Parkin isn't the only character … And this is Stella's big moment. Or it will be.'
'Doreen! Welcome back! We've just …'
'Oh, OK, then, off you go home.'
'Give me strength.'
'Yes, that's it. Goodnight, everyone! See you on Wednesday unless I've been lucky enough to be hospitalised! Bye!'
'Stella, no, no hat in this scene … We discussed it …'

THE SORT

She was the sort of person who specialised in telling other people the sort of person she was.

'I'm the sort of person who just comes out with it,' she would say. 'I'm sassy and spirited and I don't mince my words.'
Which was her way of justifying the frequent occasions on which she was spectacularly rude.
'I was just being honest,' she said, as a friend (or soon-to-be-ex-friend) wept across a restaurant table. 'I'm the sort of person who doesn't deal in bullshit.'
Which was meant to get her off the hook, we thought, while helping the soon-to-be-ex-friend to her Uber, confirming with her that, actually, her engagement ring was beautiful and bore no relation to the one in the catalogue to which I'm-the-sort had referred.
'She needed to know her husband-to-be is a cheapskate,' she said. 'I'm the sort of person who doesn't hold back when she can see the truth.'
'But what it isn't the truth?' I asked. 'What if it's just the truth as you see it? He doesn't make the sort of money you and your friends do, and you don't like him, but she loves him and he loves her and ...'

She was also the sort of person who specialised in telling other people what sort of person she considered them to be.
'You're the sort of person,' she said to me, waving the waiter away, as he hovered with the sea bass he had been about to deliver to the bride-to-be. 'You're the sort of person who likes to make excuses for people. You never have the courage to sit in judgment.'
'And you're the sort of person who does?' I replied, realising that I shouldn't have expressed this as a question, because it was, in fact, the answer.

She made the sort of shrug made by women who wear dead animals across their shoulders. 'I'm the sort of person who tells it like it is.'

'Tells it as she sees it,' I corrected her. 'Not as it is. You express an opinion as if it is a fact, but that does not make it a fact.'

'You're the sort of person who plays with words and tries to cancel free speech,' she hissed. 'The sort who …'

'The sort who calls people out for being utter …' and I completed the sentence with a word I won't write down.

'How childish,' she said. 'Such language marks you as the sort of person who …'

'… who calls out nasty, mean-minded so-called friends.'

Bride-to-be returned at this point. 'I'm so sorry,' she said to I'm-the-sort, 'I took your coat by mistake.'

She handed the coat back to its owner.

'And there I was, thinking you must be the sort of person who had lots of money, after your comments about my ring,' she said. 'Unless 'acrylic' is the new cashmere, of course …'

I'm the sort of person who takes a malicious delight in seeing people get their come-uppance. Don't judge me.

THE FOOD BANK

Abi saw the man arrive and recognised his demeanour immediately. This had to be his first visit to the food bank. Lots of people, on their first visit, had that particular body language. It communicated 'I'm not really here.'

Abi gave the man a smile and said 'Hi'.

'How does it work, then?' he asked, his face, his lips, his eyes hardly moving.

'Have you got your voucher?' she asked.

The man reached into his coat pocket and produced the printed out e-voucher, unfolding it with the fingertip delicacy of a bomb disposal expert.

Abby looked at the voucher, said 'OK,' and picked up an appropriate box. 'This has three day's worth …'

The man's eyes suddenly shifted from Abi to a point behind her. A frightened look contorted his face.

'Can I come round there?' he asked, pointing behind the counter. His mouth was doggy, wet.

Ali felt anxious, threatened. 'No,' she said.

But he moved behind the counter anyway. Ali decided that staying calm was the best option.

A man and a woman, both in heavy coats and scarves, arrived at the counter. They looked like first-timers as well.

The man in the heavy coat looked at the man next to Abi and smiled a sly, cold smile which didn't reach his eyes.

'What the fuck are you doing here?' he asked.

Abi's man shot a quick glance at her. Again, the fear.

'I'm volunteering here,' he said. 'I help out after work.'

'The fuck,' the other man said. 'You've never volunteered for anything in your life.'

'Now I have.'

The woman said, 'You've found a conscience at last.' She had the same sly, calculating look.

Abi's man told Abi 'This is my brother.'

The woman leant towards Abi. 'They haven't seen each other for years,' she said. 'No wonder, considering.'

An awkward silence.
'How does it work, then?' the brother asked. 'The food bank.'
Abi's man hesitated. Then, smoothly, 'Have you got your voucher?'
The brother, with the same pained expression Abi's man had adopted, pulled from his pocket a tightly-folded voucher.
'How many people?' asked Abi.
'Two,' the man replied. With relief, Abi turned away to organise the food parcel for the couple.
The brother, his face hard, murmured, 'The business is gone.'
Abi's man didn't move. 'Last time I saw you it was flourishing, expanding …'
'No, it wasn't. You were showing off about your fucking 'lifestyle' so I lied.'
The woman said 'You're as bad as each other.'
'And now,' said the brother, 'we've got nothing and you're Mr Virtuous, volunteering and giving us a fucking food parcel.'
'Actually,' Abi's man said. Abi turned, the food parcel ready in her hands. 'Actually, I'm not a volunteer, I'm just one ahead of you in the queue.'
Abi saw him decide. He stepped towards his brother and gave him a huge bearhug.
'I've got nothing too,' Abi's man said.
There were tears in both men's eyes.
'You haven't got nothing,' Abi said. 'You've got a brother.'

OPENING UP

Today she is at her lowest and, as always on such days, opening the curtains seems like an act of rebellion. Her mind is telling her that it makes sense to leave them closed. The sunshine making the curtains glow is harmful, her mind says; the sun is a huge, scrutinising, judgmental eye staring at her, into her. It should be kept out. Her mind is also telling her (and this isn't a 50-50 split; her mind is telling her both things at 100% intensity, forcing her to try to balance them) that opening the curtains is the best thing she can possibly do. Opening the curtains will challenge her by taking her from the comfort zone of home – in which everything but her mind is controllable – into the unpredictable, uncontrollable world; it will challenge her to look beyond herself, the benefit being that maybe, just maybe, that change of perspective will give her some strength and escape from herself.

She visualises what the outside world might be like. She saw it yesterday for a few moments, before the dust began swirling and two paper bags from the corner shop began to circle in a way she found indescribably sinister. But that was yesterday. Yesterday. Now she visualises differently, seeing herself walking, face held to the sunlight, wearing her big coat - no, not the big coat, it would blow about in the breeze and make her look chaotic, demented (she winces at using this word about herself) and unmistakeably like a woman with depression trying to cheer herself up by walking quickly on a windy, sunny day. Not the big coat. She will wear her zip-up down jacket and some jeans and some trainers and look … 'normal'. (Even in her own company, she is PC enough to add inverted commas so as to render 'normal' a term she knows she shouldn't use but can't think of a replacement for.) She's walking, her face turned up to the sunshine, wearing sunglasses (but not the huge dark glasses she used to wear to make herself feel invisible) and, yes, the endorphins are kicking in and a smile is forming and …

Is her visualization strong enough? Sometimes she gets to this point and the imagined endorphin rush is enough to motivate her to start moving quickly in order to experience it for real.
Sometimes it doesn't work. She checks in with herself and realises there is a smile on her face. The smiling muscles feel stiff, unused. Yes, she will get dressed and go for a walk. First, though …
She reaches for the curtain, holds it, regrets its slightly rough texture. (The more expensive ones were softer. But expensive. Too expensive.) She breathes - seven in, seven out (for balance). She worries, for a second, about swirling paper bags. She visualises them, tries turning them from scary circling vultures into skittering kittens, visualises herself laughing, doing a little dance. Before she can stop herself, she pulls the curtains open.

EAU DE NIL

I'm on the DLR and I've just noticed that the rather handsome man sitting opposite is wearing a zip-up polo shirt in (Google tells me; I checked) eau de nil and, perhaps more remarkably, the strap on his watch is exactly the same colour.

This leads to speculation. In his (I imagine) immaculate home, is there a wardrobe full of zip-up polos in a range of somewhat undecided colours like this one with, near to range, in a drawer that slides open with an expensive sigh, a selection of watch straps in exactly the same shades, thus allowing him to match any shirt with any strap? Is there a cerulean to go with the cerulean, a crimson with the crimson, a taupe for the taupe …?

Of course, he's gay. Only a gay man could be quite that put together, that – what's the vogue word – intentional?

The thought rebounds. Am I stereotyping? There are plenty of gay men with terrible dress sense, and isn't it exciting to see a straight man taking care of his appearance, showing enjoyment in wearing subtle colours and matching his accessories and eschewing stereotypes in order to express himself in the way that all the minorities are encouraged to do?

Yes! He is a straight man who doesn't care if strangers on the DLR instantly assume he is gay! He is brave, a rebel, a vanguard for metrosexuality and freedom from patriarchal oppression!

Of course he may be a straight man who, having chosen this outfit and combed his impossibly impeccable hair, has picked his way in nonchalant disgust over the detritus of his child's porridge-splashed toys and left his wife and said child in a welter of sleep-deprived confusion, heading for work without a backward glance, caring only for his own beauty …

I hate him. How could he treat his wife so badly?

Of course he may be a gay man with a child. Why did I assume that he had to be straight, with a child? Now my assumptions are being chased by my afterthoughts like foxes by hounds … Yes, of course, he's gay, and the parent he has left with his child is a brawny beauty in a zip-up polo just like his (Sea Salt? Avocado?) who is, as we speak, mopping vomit off his shoulder and smiling with undying love at the miracle bundle in his arms …

I love him.

Oh my God! Check my assumptions again! If he's straight, Eau de Nil's escaped a house of confusion and mess; if he's gay, the life he's left behind is as picture-perfect as he is!

I shall so have to phone Ramon when I get to work, and set up a session. All these assumptions! All these stereotypes! And I've been working so hard. I am deeply disappointed in myself.

I look at him again.

He's so matchy-matchy and perfect. Perhaps he's not so beautiful after all.

He's very annoying.

How dare he bring out the worst in me!

COMING AROUND AGAIN

He put on his standard uniform of grey chinos and grey shirt and opened the curtains, his plum-coloured sweater dangling from his hand. He looked out, speculatively. Yes, the sky was grey, but nothing immediately suggested that, outside, it was cold enough to justify wearing the sweater. He paused. He'd been caught out before. Then he spotted a man walking in the direction of his house wearing a light jacket over a shirt and chinos, looking perfectly comfortable; that decided it. He wasn't going to wear the sweater.

While checking his beard for toast crumbs (none) and his shaved head for nicks (none) he heard a soft click, then the sound of running footsteps. He loved his neighbour's children but cursed the neighbours for not having stair carpet.

He put his jacket on, left the house and headed towards the station. At the corner he stepped out from the shelter of the houses and into a cold wind which made him shiver. The sweater. He should have worn the sweater. He looked at his watch; he had time to go back and still catch the right train.

He headed back towards the house. Looking up at the bedroom window he saw what he thought at first was just the shadow of a swaying tree on the glass but, no … What he saw was a man looking out, holding his plum-coloured sweater.

There was a man in his flat! With his plum-coloured sweater! A bald, white-bearded man wearing grey chinos and a grey shirt. He started to run towards the house; the man in the window turned away.

He opened the front door as quietly as he could, slipped off his shoes and ran as lightly as he could up the stairs. He had no idea what he'd do next, so he ducked into the second bedroom to think.

The man came out of the bedroom and headed down the stairs. Not only was he wearing an identical shirt and trousers to him, he was putting on an identical jacket as he went.

He still had no idea what to do. He tiptoed into the bedroom and looked out of the window. The man was walking away from the house, down the road towards the station.

He picked up the plum-coloured jumper, not especially because it was what he'd come for, but in disbelief that that stranger had touched it. It didn't occur to him, in his bewilderment, to check and see if anything had been stolen.

At the corner, the man in the identical outfit gave a kind of shiver, looked at his watch, and headed back towards the house.
From the window, it was easy to study the man in more detail. The outfit, the beard, the bald head; it was like looking into a mirror. He peered intently then, worried that the man would see him, he turned away, putting the sweater back on the chair.

He heard a soft click, then the sound of running footsteps.

CAFFEINE AND COINCIDENCE

I've decided to write a story in exactly 500 words. Exactly 500, no more, no fewer. You can make a point in 500 words, while remaining pithy. You can be pithy and make a point.

It's a story about love. Why love? There are other stories to be told – about murders, misery, grief, poverty, illness, politics, other grim things – and those stories should be told, but there are also moments in life when we want to turn away from those stories and escape, so that when we return to 'reality', we are refreshed. OK?

So, love.

There's a man in a café reading the sort of book it is good to be seen reading in a café. He looks up and sees, across the room, a man in a tweed coat and round glasses reading – oh! – the same book. The man has a darkly stubbled chin and hairy backs to his hands and is gorgeous – not gorgeous, gorgeous, unapproachably perfect gorgeous, but nice, friendly, ordinary gorgeous. He has read, it seems, possibly fifty pages fewer of the book than our man has.

Our man, emboldened by caffeine and coincidence, stands up and takes the five steps necessary to cross the small room. The tweed coat man looks up.

'How about that?' our man says, holding out his copy of the book, his finger marking the place he'd got to (page 78, the middle of a chapter in which the story's hero describes how he met his husband).

'I'm sorry?' tweed coat man says. He doesn't look pleased. He has a line of cappuccino froth on his top lip.

Our man feels foolish. He feels like retreating five steps and turning his back in shame.

But then, then Tweed Coat catches on. 'We're reading the same book!' he says. And he smiles.

'Yes,' breathes Our Man. 'Yes. How about that?'
'How about that?' says Tweed Coat. He has wrinkles at the sides of his eyes and Our Man wants to touch them. Our Man has momentarily stopped breathing. Then, 'It's bloody awful, isn't it?'

Our Man continues not breathing. Then, 'Actually, yes,' he says. 'Apart from the bit I've just got to – '

'No spoilers,' says Tweed Coat. 'Not that there's anything to spoil.'

'It is awful,' Our Man says. 'Sort of hackneyed and dull and repetitive and full of little writer's tricks and things that only happen in books – '

'- or Richard Curtis movies –'

And Our Man glows inside because Tweed Coat didn't quote Kierkegaard or Ezra Pound or the Post-Modernists or Intersectional Feminism to make his point, he referenced someone mainstream. And he referenced that someone with a cappuccino-and-stubble-fringed smile. He has a wonky tooth that adds to his ordinary gorgeousness.

They smile at each other; a smile that has 'Hello, soul mate' in it.

Three hours later, high on caffeine, coincidence, conversation and kissing, Our Man gets home. He fires up his computer and types:

'I've decided to write a story in exactly 500 words ...'

LAYLA CURR:

C DASH DASH K

When Lenny Bruce died, alone and near destitute on the toilet, the shame he'd been forced through served to drag him further down through the dark. And into it, too, as with every blocked bowl, the shit rises, shown in how the trials and persecutions he suffered had made him, after over fifty years, a near Saint. But can jews become Saints? This was a question C. pondered, as he sat there now, on his toilet, expelling some of the bad chinese food from last night.

He thought about Lenny a lot, but then so did every Stand-Up Comic he favoured. Lenny Bruce was their Jesus and their Spartacus, too, come to that. He had paved the way down to Hell but had also set the fork in the road towards Heaven. Lenny had thrown himself to the fires: he was the jewish or Jew Joan of Arc. Everyone rose after him, everyone blazed and post-phoenixed, with lessons learnt from his language; Richard Pryor, George Carling, Bill Hicks with the cancer; it was clear that the idea of sainthood for the foul mouthed and funny had become a positively revolutionary act. C. knew that nobody would ever call him a Saint, but he had nevertheless noted down the example. He had in many ways studied the various forms of ascension and the demands it made on you, if not in himself, then through work. The strength of what he had produced recently brought him close to that state, as he had crossed and transgressed many borders, so much so, that his work and words were like soldiers, who after many long years of battle had mitigated disaster and placed him at Fifty ahead of both the field and the game.

He had recently turned fifty-one, and all of those former battles were over. A different campaign had now started, free from both bomb, or attack. Those may well come in time, gifts from women intent on revenge, or from husbands. But for now, all was peaceful and eerie as well. Suspense ruled. But not the kind of shock or, surprise, or anything close to sensation, but rather one that dread stationed, as he waited to fear what came next. This was to be a new silent war, in which he would receive no battle plan and no orders. Unless they came from a court. So, he waited behind the fragile enemy lines of his home.

As C. sat there, he thought on as he always would, about Lenny. He imagined them as friends at the Lamplight, or Gaslight, or some other small club Off Broadway, wowing them all, he at fifty and Lenny at maybe ninety-six, or, even ninety nine years of age. C. would have had to wheel Lenny on, as they did with Groucho Marx in his eighties, but they both would have made such a couple; the bald and the bold man; two little dissidents on display. If it made any difference, C. would have carried Lenny on in his arms to show the special connection between them, that's if he truly believed such an action would have convinced them again of his worth. He would have used Lenny, he knew, as the worst kind of mascot; a shield, beard, or cover, or a mask to obscure his past sin. All Bruce had done was take drugs and been a little careless with people. And yet he'd been practically crucified for it, so what were they going to do to him? A fart came. It sounded out, trumpeting; the sad song of the middle aged. C. sighed deeply. He had been fatally bound by his penis, just as Bruce was by truth. As he crouched there, staring on, an unfortunate thought kept repeating; both he and his hero had been forced out and fondled and even abused, fucked by fame.

It was going to be a similar kind of trial, or war for C. now, after what he had done, declared on him. First by all women and then in time, by most men. He would have to shoulder the blame for all sins, while being pierced in the side by opinion, but unlike another famous jew before Lenny, he could not preach forgiveness, or be seen to ask for it at all. Or, not yet. All he would be able to do now was hide, a Lazarus who's still living, stuck in his cave like apartment with all of the treasures and pleasures of the current world close to hand. Which he would have to watch constantly, as it seemed to have a life of his own. He had learned that. And yet even as he resolved to forsake masturbation, he knew in that dreamstate that all too often and always without warning, the blood would start moving, and the reality of his needs would take hold.

Why had he done it in the first place? God knew. But then God didn't exist, so that screwed him; perhaps it had been an exercise of his power, or some sort of demonstration of edge. He had never been the coolest or most accepted of kids, what with that sallow, hungry look and his lunar like leprous freckles. And of course, the red hair was a hindrance. In a Jimmy Olsen world, others flew. But after the self-deprecation and sense and pre-contracted years made of struggle, he had paid his dues and soon crafted a way for the geek to gain ground, and having found fame and repute after scaling a rung or three of the ladder he had reached a place and point of ascension, at least as he understood it, that felt authentic to many and had the potential of course to mean more. He'd met all of his heroes, made friends and over the years reached the point where he was the one that other funny people found funny. And because he was older and no longer a kid, wisdom came. And with that wisdom, some joy, or what he thought was joy; which translated into respect and attention, and then money, and fame; Pussy. Work.

His had been a typical American tale; born in the 'burbs, with its usual low-end expectations. And yet then, he had worked, won, transcended, so why not now, after so long, when it had finally come to him, celebrate? This is how he had justified it to himself, and his daily dumping ground helped review it. He had only been spreading the love and declaiming, through that little horn of his own, fame's sweet song. But then, that's the issue, or point, as we all have our own tastes in music. And what he had imagined as fanfare had quickly become requiem.

C. reached around, wiped his ass and grazed the offending item in question. Coiled, subdued, squatting, its selfishness wounded and weighed him down, hourly. It wasn't as if it was a big thing at all, but it had still packed the punch that destroyed him. Its demands on him, or his and it, had brought him here, to a place where its lack of length still tied knots that would possibly never be loosened. Hunched over, subdued, he glared at it, screaming his strange silent questions as its single aperture remained closed. It was thanks to this boneless thumb that he would continue to write without any interest, or commission. After a decade of growing worth and expansion, this retracted little worm just reduced. It saw his life stop. This thing was a proper period placed, but this time at the start of the sentence, which felt he would always be serving, as he moved from being a former man of invention to someone addicted to having women watch him jerk off.

He had never asked them to touch him, just watch. It had been a show of self he was making. Completely different of course to the Stand-up, or the One Man Show on Netflix. Or, to the Sit-com on Fox, the series on Prime, and the guest spots. In fact, in relation to those, it was either more private or perhaps more performed; special, too. Or, that's how he had seen it. He'd shared. And (dreaded word:) expressed his own limitations. The ordinary guy had gained glory. And look; here's the bugle. You don't even have to blow. I can play.

His ass was cold. His leg shook. His crap was cool at the anus. A thought that while ugly, was at best honest, and attempting to be beautiful. Which is what he had tried to do afterall, as there had been a strain of irony to his efforts; the onanist on his organ in a recital in which hands trace the movements from which sperm's particular sounds start to sing.

As he considered it all he changed the scene, still creating. His bathroom would now become courtroom as toothbrush, shampoo and aftershave became Jury. The cistern was judge; towels, attorneys, and with the closed door as Clerk, standing guard. Why he had closed the door, no-one knew, as he was now alone. It was habit. And something only goys did; hence Lenny, dead for all to see on his john. C. was shielding himself as he shat, trying to free the crap in him. Or, perhaps it was more than that; this was ritual, a cleansing that came with great effort, albeit with rejection as the ultimate price. He still owed.

He sweated a little. He strained. He thought about P's pretty face, folding, creased by her intense disapproval. He'd watched her at the time, as her gorgeous eyes narrowed, and he had felt sick to his stomach when that wonderfully kissable mouth found its sneer. And this from a woman he'd loved and who he had worked with so closely. He had given her the moon in his series, in what was still a standout for all seasons, as well as, sincerely, the most romantic thing he had made.

When she had hung up that last time, he had felt the guillotine fall and grave open. Even in the Summer heat she had chilled him, with the hatred that roared through her words. It wasn't even the act. It was the standards they'd set she was grieving. He had betrayed their two-person campaign against bullshit to make comedic truth art's new grain. And all for what? One more come, that momentary rush most men live for. One more small explosion that weakens the ground with each burst. Men will always wear themselves out. P. said that. Its why they keep their ramshackle cars going, or only buy new clothes when their old ones are practically haunting their back, feet, or ass. Its why they eat long passed its sell by date food, and as they're going bald, try comb-overs. Men are basically driftwood dealers while women of course, are the stream. Now C. was sat on the banks, and so very far from warm water. P. was his pal, girl, his partner, his source and his sea. She'd swum on.

And yet he had never touched, never forced. He had only ever asked the women he'd met, or been with. Though, at times, he'd implored them. If anything, he thought that he had resembled a child on the potty calling to his replacement mothers to look, or to check. He'd been proud. His had been a soliloquy set apart and at the appropriate distance, and composed from a particular flame roused inside him, as well as outside; a flicked switch, which had suddenly shone a new light on what others now thought and had possibly expected before this. It had started as a joke; penis preening. But then it had quickly become a compulsion; a signature of sorts, made from skin.

There was no defence. The towels glared and remained blank faced, closed, unyealding. The toothpaste and brush glared right past him. The shampoo remained resolute. The toilet below chasmed down, to become an abyss sent to snare him, just as it had once been to Lenny, who in his last fear-stained moments, must have heard the underworld itself calling him.

He imagined Lenny now, if he'd lived, and what he might have been; still a comic? Or, perhaps a memoir guy, or headwriter on a series about his career. There had been something like that on Prime, inspired he thought by Joan Rivers, but Lenny would have made his series and books and plays like The Wire, but with funnier jokes. Or just jokes. C. imagined Bruce old, and walking into the show he'd just finished. An old guy at the bar, wise but bitter about the state of all things, free to blame. But with a sparkle there still, to balance the part played by Alda. Those two guys there together would have been something to see: M*A*S*H meets dashed (----).

Lenny Bruce would certainly have laughed this off in his prime, but C. had now lost all sense and all humour. The women he'd loved would now hate him, not just for being a prick, or his actions, but for the worst of all possible letdowns; for not being the person that everyone had thought he was, or might be. What we are, or are not no-one knows, which is in the end, the frustration and charm, to most people, and yet now for C. things were different. A crueler criteria was applied.

What are the specific degrees of your crime? And to what extent are your helpless? And how does one measure intention against the rate and range of affect? The women would be asked, interviewed, and the judgements applied in an instant. Privacy had been violated. He would be a symptom and stain; a new wound.

In the wake of Spacey, and Weinstein, all this: a charged, callous climate in which every accusation felt equal. There would be no way to countermand or to argue that what he had done was less harmful than any other predatory claim on soft skin. He was Roger

Ailes, Jeffrey E. And maybe even that weird DJ guy in England. So, who would stand by, or speak for him? And what about his male friends? No-one had called. It had been a month. Social lockdown. Chris, Jerry, Larry, Jeff, Marc, Ricky: who, why and when? He mouthed each name to the room, but as it was thickly tiled, gained no echo. The sound was as dead as his efforts to try and regain currency.

What are men, anyway, but beasts full of burden? The Rolling Stones said it and he a hummed a bar of the song as he thought. Men spend as much of their lives as they can trying to shift the weight that's thrust on them, which is clearly the result of expectation, genetics, and society, too, in full sway. But as soon as they fail at it they're damned and cast aside. They're dispensed with. They get their chance then it's over. The day's plant dies. The next's grows. There was clearly no line to be saved, no connecting thread, just sad anchors, rotting away at the bottom of the sea or split harbour, with the boats they had once secured long since sailed.

C. coughed, cleared his throat and spat in the basin beside him. No-one he'd ever known had succeeded. It was all attempts that led nowhere, or towards degrees of descent in his case. He resolved to try to write it all out, set it down and plot a new course, like a series. The one he'd just done had been perfect, a blending of theatre and truth and TV. But this was a new challenge: a new film that could be experienced and seen on the street, and in theatres. He would remake himself as a sequel. Perhaps that was his private path out of this.

What would Lenny have done? Well, you didn't need to ask: Lenny did it. His last appearances featured transcripts of his perennial trials and routines. He was throwing up his own life, while sweating the last of his soul through a raincoat. He was turning to dust and then dying. Did C. have to die too, for his sins?

Suicide wouldn't work. He was a better writer than that, free from cliché. And in those better times, still so frequent the search for new modes was the aim. That's what his work was about: the part, or piece in you that strives, or continues. It was a point of principle, that no matter how vapid, or how fruitless it seems, you go on. One moment heralds the next, that's the arc; shit, or shot, something of quality, or unworthy. And until you are dead. That plot's written, but the details, and movements are always going to be yours to fill out.

He felt a surge of energy, saw a goal: He would write his way back to acceptance. He would try to explain to those women what an asshole he'd been with his prick. It was a sad celebration, pitiable, but originally meant as a self-defeating joke from the body. He had been trying to say its all bullshit; from male neurosis, through the expectations of sex, love and beauty, to some other level, or plain where it stops mattering as to who, or what is attractive. The ridiculousness would be worth it. Afterall, dogs find other dogs sexy. The face has no function and so body at best is a game. You just needed to find the right players, that's all; kindred cocks, cunts, and counters. It wasn't about coercion, oppression, or any other abuse of male power; it was all instead, chaos, which is just a comedic take on distraction, or, what former comic friends of his might define as what slapstick is, or was to Mort Sahl.

He would write about his mother, his wife, and the pressure Dads feel from their daughters. He would write about girls and girlfriends and headmistresses, too, teachers, dreams. He would write about the need to forgive and the appeasements within human weakness and the fact that there could be no forgiveness, as to forgive and forget is divine. It has no end to it, and no range. Or, rather no start, as those who truly forgive become angels. They transcend human values and most human behaviour, as well. They are Gods. Man and womankind can never truly forgive, or excuse, but they can adapt, accept, alter. As a matter of fact, if people all had a mind to, they could grant even mindlessness some small worth.

He stood up shakily, inviting the blood in his legs back to colour. He looked at his shy boy's face in the mirror and looked down at his dick, shameful, small. He toppled slightly, and placed a freckled hand on the basin. He wiped himself, flushing Lenny, who sang spiralling all the way down past the rim.

The shower spoke to his skin and he willed himself into the kitchen and breakfast. Coffee he knew couldn't cure him, but it could at least bring resolve. He scrambled some eggs, filled his cup and sat once more at a table. He turned his computer on, started writing. What was left of the dawn inked grey cloud.

When they axed this last series he knew that his idea of God had died with it, and then after God, Woody Allen, or the idea of his first comic hero, whom he had always wanted to be, would fall dashed. And yet he had wanted that body of work, if not in scope, then in scale, as he had so many films in him, so many plays, notions, novels, and many more TV series of course. And then of course, there was all of the Stand-Up stood down on account of the scandal. But what his dick had damned he would salvage, even if of course no-one read. Which is what Woody Allen had said years ago when asked what he'd do if people stopped wanting his movies: to which he'd replied he would simply carry on writing, just setting it down for himself.

C. rallied, slightly. He sniffed, then sipped at the vapour tapering coffee. He would apologise to all women and then to himself, every day. It would be a continuing series of scenes that he and the spirit of Lenny were writing, detailing the mistakes of men at all junctures, and the quandaries made to confront them which each in their own way would potentially try to resolve. The work would be simple and true and have no guile at all. He'd be honest. And this in itself made him happy. He would write it all down and keep going and in so doing would construct no device and thereby actively surrender his talent. It was a sacrifice: his bad sentence, the price that he at last had to pay. As he typed without pause, he started to get an erection. He let out a brief howl of laughter.

Outside, a gentle thunderclap echoed as the grey clouds swelled. The rain came.

Printed in Great Britain
by Amazon

23563585R00126